Cloudberry Castle

Janey Louise Jones

 Kelpies

For Katie Mackenzie, with love

Kelpies is an imprint of Floris Books

First published in 2010 by Floris Books
© 2010 Janey Louise Jones
Illustrations © 2010 Moira Munro

British Library CIP data available
ISBN 978-086315-765-3
Printed in Great Britain by JF Print Ltd.

1. Christmas at Cloudberry

It was Christmas Eve last year. I was sitting on my bedroom floor in Holly Cottage, wrapping presents for my family. I had been saving up some of my weekly pocket money since the summer, and Mum took me into Perth to do Christmas shopping. For my five-year-old sister, Sorcha, I had bought a dressing-table mirror surrounded by shells and mermaids. It was really pretty, but a bit tricky to wrap! As for Hamish, what *can* you get for a three-year-old boy? Mum helped me to decide. I wrapped the two "knights on horseback" figures for him, both wearing suits of armour. One of the horses had a kind face and the other looked mean. A goodie and a baddie, which is just what he likes.

For Mum and Dad, I had made a big memory box all about our family, the Mackenzies, and our life here on the beautiful Cloudberry estate. Mum was always worrying that she couldn't find her favourite little family things, so I thought it would be good to put everything special together. I had painted the outside of the box with amber-coloured cloudberries, dark green fir trees and purple heather — all the varied colours of Cloudberry. *Thank goodness I don't have to wrap this one!* I thought, as the box was quite big.

My grannies and grandpas all love Scrabble, and they said they had lost a few tiles, so I got that game for the Mackenzies from Edinburgh and the Berrys from Boston, USA. Easy-peasy to wrap! And finally, for old Dr Campbell up in the castle, I had made some chocolate truffles, which were in a shiny gold box I had saved from last Christmas.

It's such fun preparing for Christmas! I love the way it gets really dark so early in wintertime. I had switched on the fairy lights around my bed, and a little lamp as well. My attic bedroom is really tiny, but I love it so much! The walls are painted a brilliant colour, which Mum found in Mr Morrison's hardware store down in Lochvale village. It's called Crushed Cranberries. Not red, not pink, not purple. Just right. The bed has a patchwork cover which Granny Mackenzie made for me when I first moved out of my cot. I've got a white wardrobe and a cupboard which used to be for toys (not any more, obviously — it's now full of ballet outfits, shoes and handbags), and a huge ballet mirror and barre. Ballet is my only hobby. I want to be a prima ballerina, like Mum used to be.

The dressing table is at the window and it's crammed full with lip balms, hairbrushes, jewellery and nail polish. I like to try out new ballet buns at the mirror all the time, but my best ones are always on the days I *don't* have ballet! Then when I go to sleep, even though I plan to lie completely still and keep the bun in place, it always goes wonky by morning.

I was very happy with my wrapping. It looked so colourful. A couple of weeks before, Mum had bought lots of plain brown paper down at Mrs Renton's post office. I had decorated it at the kitchen table the week before Christmas with red, green and gold paint. My best design was the gold stars — all sizes, with dots of colour in between. I tied red ribbons round all the parcels and made some tags from leftover paper. I wrote messages to everyone in my gold pen and attached the tags to the ribbons. There! The presents were all done. Ready to put under the tree in the family room alongside all the other gifts which had appeared over the last week.

I got up and stretched, then stood at the barre and did a couple of pliés. I looked at myself in the mirror. I had grown such a lot in the last year. And I'd got thinner too, even though I was eating loads. My brown hair was in its usual shoulder-length bob. My eyes are quite big and round, but they'd look so much better with eyeliner. Mum doesn't agree. I decided to get my make-up bag from my dressing table and experiment.

That was when I looked out of my window. The night was pitch black by now, not just a bit dark like it gets in towns and cities, where the street lamps glow here and there. I mean really, really dark, as if black velvet had been laid over the whole world. I'm used to that, but something looked different from usual. At first, I couldn't think what it was, then I realised — there were no lights on up in Cloudberry Castle.

The castle stands on a hill above our little cottage. It has four fairy-tale towers and a big clock tower in the middle, which always reads two o'clock. The date 1856 is carved into the main tower, so that's when it must have been built.

In winter, Dr Campbell, the owner, always sat in the library with a log fire burning and a few small lamps on. They were usually on by this time. Sometimes I could just make him out, prodding the fire with a long stick. Then he'd settle down again on his armchair, with a tartan blanket round his legs and a notebook and pen in his hands. I guessed he was writing about ancient Egypt — his favourite subject.

Occasionally, I saw him taking a key from behind the

clock on the mantelpiece. He would use it to open a little cupboard, hidden in the wooden panels by the fireplace.

He never went anywhere. A supermarket van came down the estate road with food shopping every few days, while Mum and Dad took in everything else he needed. I loved to go up with Mum when she took homemade broth or a rack of freshly baked fruit scones. The castle seemed to be enchanted, and it always made me want to dance through the corridors as if I was Cinderella at the ball in a wonderful white silk dress, covered in rosebuds ...

At other times, I would just pass by the castle when I was checking on Bella, the estate's Shetland pony. In summer, she's always grazing in the meadow behind the castle, beside the shimmering Lily's Lake. In winter, she lives in a stable in the mews, where all the horses and carriages used to be kept when the castle was first built. Bella doesn't belong to me, or to anyone in particular. We can't remember when she first arrived here, but we make sure she is well fed and shod.

The thing about Cloudberry until that Christmas was that, even though the seasons brought their changes in the weather and the scenery, nothing else really changed at all. Everything was always the same, day after wonderful day, which is why I thought it was so strange that I couldn't see any signs of Dr Campbell on Christmas Eve.

"Mum!" I called as I ran down to the kitchen. "The castle is completely dark. Dr Campbell might have had an accident!"

2. The Fawn

The kitchen smelled of bread sauce, which was cooking gently on the stove. The cloves filled the air with a lovely spicy aroma. Mum was working at the kitchen sink, washing carrots and Brussels sprouts, while Dad was peeling potatoes at the table. He walks with a stick, since he had his accident. It happened when we lived in the city when I was tiny, and I can't remember much about it. He likes to do sitting-down jobs around the house. It's the same with his main job, actually. He writes reports all about food and restaurants for magazines. Sitting in the car going to restaurants, sitting in restaurants eating meals, sitting at his computer writing about restaurants. Luckily he isn't a very big eater, otherwise he'd probably be enormous with all that food and not much exercise!

Sorcha was standing on a chair at the other side of the big wooden table, piling mincemeat from a jar into little star and love-heart pastry cases on a baking tray. Hamish was lying in front of the stove on the cherry-red rug, with a whole load of cars lined up for a race.

"Mum, d'you know if Dr Campbell's okay?" I asked breathlessly. "Are we still going to see him tomorrow morning?" We always went to wish him a merry Christmas on Christmas morning. Mum, Dad and our grandparents drank sherry and ate slices of very old fruit cake, while we ran about the castle, exploring the towers. Bliss! It was the best part of Christmas.

"Oh, Katie. I only heard this afternoon," began Mum. "I'm afraid Dr Campbell has been taken into a special nursing home."

"What? Is he ill?" I asked.

"Yes, he needs to have proper medical attention. He's not been eating much and he's a bit frail," she said.

"But you take him lots of meals. And the van brings his food. He was in the library just last night. Is he coming back soon?" I asked, feeling very confused. Old Dr Campbell couldn't go away for Christmas! It was a *tradition* that we saw him.

"He might be back. We don't know. Let's see how he gets on, shall we? We can visit him on Boxing Day if you like — at The Rowans. It's just a couple of miles away," said Mum.

The Rowans? I'd seen that sign by the roadside before, on the way to Perth. I was sure it was the sort of place where old people go forever and ever.

"I would really like to see him. I've got a present for him," I said.

"Well, let's do that then," said Mum. "He'll enjoy that."

"And we can take him mince pies too," suggested Sorcha.

"Yes, of course we can," agreed Mum, taking the bread sauce off the heat, and checking on some bread she was baking in the oven. "Now, who's coming out to the garden with me to collect greenery and berries? We can spray some of them gold. All the grannies and grandpas will be here in a few hours. We've got to make the place look gorgeous!"

"Yeah!" said Sorcha and Hamish, running to get their anoraks and wellies.

"Are you coming, Katie?" asked Mum, flicking on the switch by the back door for the garden lights.

"Yes, okay. I'll get my boots and jacket," I agreed. I usually love this job with the greenery, and can't wait to see my grannies and grandpas, especially Mum's parents, the Berrys, who come all the way from America. But I was feeling very worried about Dr Campbell. Imagine not being in your own home at Christmas. I wondered when Mum had been planning to tell me, if I hadn't spotted that the castle was in darkness.

"Cheer up, darling!" said Dad, as I sat by the stove, slowly pulling on my dotty wellies. "Wait until you see what Father Christmas brings you!"

I smiled. "It's just that I like everything to be the *same* every Christmas, Dad," I explained. "We *always* go up to the castle."

"I know, I know. None of us likes change, Katie. But things do change, sweetheart. I used to have two good legs and now I don't. But let's think about all the lucky things, eh? We've got a lovely home, and we've got each other," he said.

I nodded. "Love you, Dad," I called over my shoulder as I ran down to the bottom of the garden, where the fir trees lead into Cloudberry's magical woodland.

As I placed some bright red holly berries in a basket, I noticed a flake of snow in the air.

"Snow!" called Hamish. "I can throw snowballs in the morning!"

"Yeah, but don't have a tantrum if someone throws one back at you, Hamish Mackenzie!" I laughed.

"I hope all our visitors arrive before the snow gets heavy," said Mum.

She went inside with the greenery, but we played in the garden for ages.

"Let's make a sleigh," suggested Hamish. "I'll be Father Christmas! And you two can be my helper elves!"

Sorcha went into the woods to gather twigs and berries to decorate our "sleigh", while Hamish and I scouted round the sheds and outbuildings, searching for larger pieces of wood and old wheels from our ancient bicycles.

As the snow got heavier, Sorcha came running over to fetch us. "Come over here!" she whispered. "But don't make a sound."

We followed her silently into the trees. I gasped. A baby deer was standing there, looking over at us. He looked very young and nervous. His beautiful big brown eyes expressed his fear. We wanted to get closer to him, but we knew we couldn't. He'd get even more scared.

"He must be lost," I whispered. At that moment, he looked up through the snowflakes to the stars, then took off into the darkness, and almost seemed to fly up into the night sky.

"Did you see where he went, Katie?" asked Sorcha.

"I think he's gone to help Father Christmas," I said.

"Wow!" gasped Hamish.

"Come on in now," I said. "Let's see what's for tea!"

As I strolled up the garden, I looked through the big window into the back of Holly Cottage. It looked so bright and warm, with candles burning and the log-burning stove glowing. I could smell the baking bread in the air. The kitchen opens into the family room, and the fairy on the Christmas tree sparkled beautifully between our squashy, bright pink velvet sofas. Mum and Dad were chatting on one of the sofas. Mum looked lovely, as usual, with her dark hair tied back in a ponytail, and a big, easy smile on her lips. Dad looked extremely scruffy in his threadbare brown jumper and ripped jeans (not ripped in a fashionable way). But he has a very kind face.

Before I switched off the garden lights, I turned to look at the castle behind me. It was just a dark outline against the night sky.

3. Surprises

"Thank you so much, Mum and Dad!" I cried, as we all sat by the tree in our pyjamas the next morning. "This is the best present *ever*!"

"Thought you'd be happy," said Dad. "I'm just glad I don't have to go!"

It was tickets to see the ballet of *Swan Lake* at Covent Garden in London on the 16th of January — danced by my favourite ballerina, Anya Swarovsky. Mum and I were going on a plane from Edinburgh with Sorcha, and we were going to stay in a hotel overnight.

"That sounds like a dream come true!" said Granny Berry. "I'm so jealous."

"I wish you could come with us," I said. I don't have a favourite grandparent, but I'm most like Granny Berry.

"So do I," she said, getting her camera in action.

"Smile and hold up the tickets, darling," she said. "I want to remember this moment. Tickets to your first ballet!"

It was a sparkly white Christmas Day, with fresh snow covering the ground. Inside Holly Cottage, there was a feeling of warmth and excitement. Sorcha and Hamish were much less bother than normal, as there was so much to play with. Everyone liked the gifts I gave them, and Mum was especially thrilled with the memory box, but I missed Dr Campbell a lot on Christmas Day.

After lunch, Grandpa Berry and I went up to the stables to see if Bella was okay. Grandpa brought a bag of carrots.

The Berrys come to see us quite often, even though they have a long way to travel. Sometimes they make a big holiday out of it and tour around Britain, or even Europe. They usually get picked up at Edinburgh airport by Grandpa Mackenzie, and all our grandparents drive up to see us together.

"You all right, Katie?" asked Grandpa as we passed the castle. "You're awful quiet. Growin' up fast, aren't you?"

Despite the fact that I was wearing a woollen coat and a hat, scarf and gloves, I shivered.

"It's just that I can't stop worrying about Dr Campbell," I explained. "He must be so confused and lonely. I don't know why he had to go away over Christmas."

"Yeah, it's real sad," agreed Grandpa. "But think of

it this way, darling. At least he'll be cosy and warm in the home, and they'll bring him hot food and cups of tea galore, won't they? I bet they'll be singing Christmas carols, playing party games … he might just love it!"

"I suppose you might be right," I said, thinking of how cold Dr Campbell always looked when he was huddled close to the fire in the library, with his blanket round his legs.

"Katie, Katie, Katie. You carry so much responsibility on your little shoulders … always worrying," said Grandpa.

We unbolted the top of Bella's stable door. She came charging over, even though she's so tiny that she can only just see over it.

"Hey, Bella," I said, digging into the bag for carrots. "Christmas lunch is served."

Once we'd made her cosy and comfortable, we crunched through the snow back to Holly Cottage.

"Let me see you dance," said Grandpa.

"Out here in the snow?" I asked.

"Yep. I'm gonna imagine you're the Christmas fairy."

I danced through the fir trees, thinking of happy Christmases in the past.

When I saw Dr Campbell at The Rowans the next day, I thought he seemed very sad. Mum went away to give the nurses some of his bits and pieces, as well as soup, Sorcha's mince pies and other goodies left over from Christmas lunch.

I gave him the truffles.

"Thank you, dear. They look delicious," he said.

"Are you okay in here?" I asked him.

"Hard to say. I reckon I've had my last Christmas at Cloudberry, that's for sure," he said. "This place will bore me to death."

"Don't say that, Dr Campbell," I said. "Why don't you write in one of your notebooks?"

"No, there's nobody interested in what I write any more," he said.

"I'll bring you back a present from London," I said, trying to cheer him up.

He nodded. "London, eh? Now don't you stay down there, mind. And don't go spending your pennies on me. You know something, Katie, you're more like my family than my family," he said.

"From now on, you will be my official third Grandpa," I told him.

He laughed with watery eyes. Then he got more serious.

"Katie, there's something I want to tell you," he said, looking round to see if Mum was in the room. "It's a secret."

"I love secrets, and I'm really good at keeping them," I replied.

"That's what I thought. Now, there's a gold key on the mantelpiece in the library at Cloudberry ..." he began.

"Which opens the cupboard hidden in the wooden panels ..." I added.

"Yes," he laughed, shaking his head in surprise. He didn't ask how I knew about it. And he didn't say what was in the cupboard. He changed the subject, and seemed a bit cheerier after that.

Mum came to join us. Dr Campbell and I played a game of draughts, while Mum flicked through a magazine called *The People's Friend.* I didn't want to leave when the bell finally rang.

"Don't eat all the truffles at once!" I said. I gave him a really long hug when we left.

"Katie, don't ever stop dancing," he said.

Once we were outside, I ran to the window of his room and pressed my nose against it. He looked over and laughed.

When all the fun and games of Christmas were over, and our two sets of grandparents left Cloudberry, I went back to school in Lochvale. Everything seemed really dull. Thank goodness for ballet! The lessons started up again in the church hall, and my best friend Mallie Lennox and

I were determined to improve. But on the second lesson of the new year, Mrs Miller, our lovely teacher, had some surprising news for us.

"Girls, I have something to tell you," she said at the end of the lesson. We all sat down cross-legged in front of her in a semicircle. She was very dainty, with her curly brown hair tied in a ribbon, and her kind eyes looking out earnestly towards us.

"I have some good news and some bad news," she began. "The good news is that we have the Perth Theatre booked for our annual show at the end of April. It's the first time we have had such an amazing venue, so I'm planning to put on a spectacular production — of *Swan Lake*!"

We all cheered. I felt a rush of excitement. My favourite ballet. The one I was going to see in London, starring Anya Swarovsky. This was very exciting news.

"And the other thing I have to tell you is that after the show, I will be leaving Lochvale," she explained.

"Oh no!" we all said at once.

"Why are you leaving, Mrs Miller?" asked Mallie.

"My husband has got a new job in Australia," she told us. "But let's all think about the show. I want it to be magnificent. New costumes, headdresses, pointe shoes for some of us," she said.

"But Mrs Miller, after the show, who will teach us?" I asked.

"Katie, the honest answer is that I don't know just yet. But we'll find someone, I'm sure," she replied.

This was another unexpected change in my life. Of course, it was lovely to think about the production of *Swan Lake* in the Perth Theatre, but after that, what would happen?

I don't like January much. The trees were all twiggy and bare, and it wasn't frosty and sparkly any more, but damp and dull. I longed for something wonderful and magical to happen to lift my spirits.

Granny Mackenzie called us up one evening to see how we were doing.

"I'm really fed up, Granny," I informed her.

"Ah. The thing about January is that you have to do all the jobs you don't get round to when the weather is nice. Sort out your wardrobe, practise your dancing, write up your diary — and it will soon be time for your trip to the ballet in Covent Garden."

"I know. I can't wait for that," I replied.

I did as Granny suggested and kept myself busy in my room, colour coding my clothes and accessories, and planning what clothes I'd take to London. But the trip couldn't come quickly enough. I marked off the days on my new calendar, and finally the 15th of January arrived. It was time to pack my case.

"We'll only be in the hotel for one night," said Mum when she saw the huge selection of stuff I had laid out on my bed. "So we don't need too much. And we're not allowed much baggage on the flight, remember, darling."

I wanted to take *all* my dresses and hair things and shoes. I didn't know what mood I'd be in before the ballet. It would have been awful if I wanted to wear something that was back at Cloudberry. But I settled on one dress which Granny Berry gave me for Christmas. It's purple velvet, with a full, short skirt with netting underneath. It looks nice with warm, turquoise tights and cosy, fur-lined boots. Sorcha and I were both taking our velvet coats.

On the morning of the 16th, we all piled into the car and Dad drove us to the airport in Edinburgh.

"What will you and Hamish do while we're away?" I asked on the way.

"Dad says we're going to go to a car-racing track!" revealed Hamish. I looked at Mum. I guessed it was the first she'd heard about it.

"I can't wait to see London," I said, changing the subject. "And I hope we have time to go shopping. I want to get something really nice for Dr Campbell."

It was quite sad saying goodbye to Dad and Hamish in the car park at the airport. Much as they annoy me at times, it doesn't feel the same when we're not all together.

"Why can't you come?" asked Sorcha as she held on to Dad.

"A few reasons, sweetheart. Firstly, there's the fact that I can't walk around a big city as fast as you lot. And secondly, there's this problem I have with ballet. For some reason, five minutes of ballet seems more like five hours to me."

"It's a miracle we ever got together, Dan," laughed Mum. "We don't have anything in common really."

Mum was a brilliant ballerina in New York, and Dad went out there one time to cook in a New York restaurant, and they met in this little deli off Fifth Avenue called Alf's. That was long before the accident. I remember he told me that he pretended to love ballet at first, just to impress Mum.

Dad looked a bit hurt. "We've got plenty in common, haven't we?"

"Of course we do," said Mum, hugging Dad. "I'm only teasing. We both love living in the middle of the countryside, and for some reason we both love these three pesky kids."

"Yeah, they're not too bad, are they? I think we'll keep them a bit longer," teased Dad.

Mum was really upset about leaving Hamish, and he

did look adorable, standing there with his blond curls and huge blue eyes. But we had to check in and go through security.

"Byeee!" we called as we entered the terminal building. "Remember to check on Bella for me," I added.

The ballet adventure had begun!

4. Dancing Dreams

Three hours later we were right in the heart of London. It was so noisy and busy. We got a black cab from Victoria railway station to our hotel, which was called Edwards. Mum chose it because it's very close to the theatre in Covent Garden. It seemed to take us ages to get there as there were traffic jams everywhere. I had never seen so many cars, or such crazy driving. *Toot! Beep! Oi!* They just didn't care. No one does that sort of driving in sleepy old Perthshire.

We paid the driver — who was so chatty about football and the fact that Scottish people drink too much whisky that we got a bit tired listening to him — and we walked up some shiny marble steps into Edwards. A revolving door was spinning and we all jumped into one section and were fired out the other side into the amazing reception area.

It was just like stepping back in time. There was a huge, sparkling chandelier in the middle of the room, with a massive table under it, which had a glass vase of fresh white lilies on top.

"Smells so nice!" breathed Sorcha.

I nodded. We held hands as Mum stood in a short queue at the reception desk, waiting to check us in. The desk was made from cherry wood, and there were beautiful paintings on the striped walls behind it.

"This is the fanciest place I've ever been in," I whispered to Sorcha.

"'Cept for our castle!" she replied, quite loudly, which made everyone stare at us.

"Shoosh, Sorcha!" I said. "It's not *our* castle!"

"Shoosh yourself," said Sorcha, who hates being told off.

After Mum had completed all the paperwork, a man in a smart suit took our bags away in one of the lifts, while we got in the other, all the way up to the third floor. Room 312. Mum swiped the key card and the green light flashed. She opened the door and Sorcha and I ran in.

"Oh, it's lovely!" I cried. Our room had three single beds in it, but it wasn't a squeeze; there was loads of space between them. We had plum-coloured satin curtains, and the bed covers matched. There was a television, a bowl of fruit and bottles of spring water. Our bags arrived, and after Mum gave the man a tip, she flopped on her bed and called Dad on the mobile phone. Meanwhile Sorcha and I investigated the bathroom supplies and all the other dinky wee things.

"See these little cartons of milk!" said Sorcha.

"Ooh! A minibar! It has chocolate in it. And there's a hairdryer," I said.

"There's a hairdryer in the minibar? Let me see!" said Sorcha.

"No, it's in the dressing-table drawer, silly!" I said.

It was as if we'd never seen these things before. And as for the writing paper with the hotel's address at the top — I *love* things like that.

"Mum, can I write to Granny Mackenzie and Dr Campbell?" I asked.

"I don't see why not," said Mum. "I've got a few stamps in my purse. We'll get home before the letters, but not to worry."

Sorcha drew some pictures of aeroplanes, while I wrote the letters.

Mum laid out our clothes for the ballet on one of the beds.

"Oh look, an ironing board," she said.

"Cool!" I said. Usually, at Holly Cottage, I hated the sight of an ironing board, but everything seemed so extra lovely in Edwards. It seemed as if it would be impossible for the room to get untidy, as everything had its own special place.

"We'll go down for tea at five," said Mum. "Then we'll walk to the Royal Opera House. It's just along the street."

We had fun getting ready. It was actually nice not to have Dad moaning at us for taking so long. The restaurant in the hotel was lovely, and I looked at it very carefully as I knew Dad would ask all about it. We had the nicest fish and chips ever, with wedges of lemon, tiny peas, crispy salad and loads of tangy mayonnaise which Mum called tartare sauce. I couldn't finish it all, but I still had space for a third share of a massive slice of hot chocolate fudge cake, with scrumptious, melty vanilla ice cream.

I couldn't wait to get to the ballet. By the time we walked out on to the street, Sorcha and I were wrapped up in our cosy new dresses, velvet coats and berets. It wasn't nearly as cold as Cloudberry, but it was a bit chilly. Sorcha always likes to dress the same as me and I don't mind that much. She's very cute, with a button nose and big brown eyes. Much prettier than me, I think. Mum says we're equally pretty. She took a photo of us leaving the hotel and sent it to Dad on her phone. I held hands with my little sister all the way along Bow Street.

I gasped when we arrived at the Royal Opera House. Apparently, it has been there since 1732. At the front of it, there's a statue called *Young Dancer*. I stared at it for ages, then I turned and looked at all the pillars on the Opera House, which were lit up from above. Hundreds of people were piling inside, showing their tickets and being shown where to go.

"Imagine how Anya Swarovsky must be feeling now," I said to Mum. "It must be amazing to be such a great dancer that all these people want to see you in action."

She nodded — she knows exactly how that feels.

We went inside and were shown to our seats, which were right at the front of the balcony. I was glad Hamish wasn't with us. He would have dangled over the edge of it.

"Mum, can you just remind us of the *Swan Lake* story again?" I asked.

"Remember, the lovely Princess Odette is turned into a swan by an evil sorcerer, Baron Von Rothbart," said Mum.

"Oh yeah, I remember. And the sorcerer makes his own daughter, Odile, seem just like Odette," I said.

"That's right. Oh, I remember when I danced Odette at the Lincoln Centre with the New York City Ballet. I was so proud, even though my feet bled and my legs ached, night after night. And when I got great reviews in the newspapers ..." I love it when Mum speaks about her life as a ballerina. I've seen photographs of her on stage and she looks so graceful and elegant.

But as Mum was recalling her dancing days, the lights went down, the orchestra struck up, and the red velvet curtains swished open. The glittering scene on the stage, of a twenty-first birthday party at a royal palace, took me to another world, and I was glued to my seat for the next two hours.

"Oh no!" I whispered into the air as I watched Odette die at the end. It seemed so real to me, and so heart-breakingly tragic. We were the last to leave our seats, as I wanted to take in the atmosphere for as long as possible.

"I *really* want to be a famous ballerina, Mum," I said as we walked back to the hotel. "It's what I want more than anything. And one day, I will dance *Swan Lake* at the Royal Opera House!"

"Well, it's a hard life, darling, but if it's what you want, then I'll give you all the help I can," Mum replied with a smile. "You never know, maybe Mrs Miller will give you the main part in your big show in April!"

I secretly hoped that would be the case, but didn't dare set my heart on it. I would do my best and even if I was just in the *corps de ballet*, I would still be happy.

When we got back to Edwards, we practically had to carry Sorcha up to the room as she was so tired. But I was wide awake. I read the brochure about *Swan Lake* again and again. The music was written by the Russian composer Tchaikovsky and it was first performed at the

Bolshoi Theatre in Moscow in 1877. I stared at the lovely photos of all the ballerinas. Anya looked so beautiful. If only Mum would let me wear make-up. *I hope Mrs Miller lets us wear make-up when we perform* Swan Lake *in Perth,* I thought.

When Mum told me to put the light out, I fell fast asleep and dreamed that I was Princess Odette, dancing through the rooms of Cloudberry Castle in my ballet shoes, searching for someone who was missing.

5. The Voice

"But Dr Campbell *can't* be dead!" I wailed. Dad had picked us up at Edinburgh airport and told us the sad news as we approached the Forth Road Bridge on the way back to Cloudberry.

"I'm so sorry to spoil your lovely time away, darling," said Dad. "It happened last night and the matron at the nursing home called me this morning. I thought you should know. He's in a better place. Try not to feel sad — remember all the funny and happy times we had with him."

Mum looked very sad, but not completely surprised by the news.

"I wonder why the people at The Rowans called us?" asked Mum, thinking aloud.

"Seemingly Dr Campbell named us as his next of kin when he arrived there," said Dad.

"How strange. Does that mean we have to inform his family?" said Mum.

"I'm not sure I'd know how to get in touch with them," Dad replied. "Where do they live?"

"Kensington in London, I think. We did meet them once, didn't we — one summer, not long after we arrived at the cottage? I think a son came to stay at the castle with his wife and young children. But there haven't been any visitors recently," said Mum. "It's all rather awkward."

Awkward? I wanted to tell Mum that it was tragic, devastating, heart-breaking. I couldn't believe she simply found it *awkward.*

Hamish wanted to tell us all about the fun he and Dad had been having while we were away.

"We saw racing cars. They went VVVvrrrroooooom!" he said, running a new toy car over the edge of his car seat.

I wasn't too interested in racing cars, but Sorcha asked Hamish some questions, which seemed to keep him happy. I pressed my head against the car window. I really wanted to bang it against the glass; I was so upset and frustrated. I felt furious that no one in the family understood how sad I was. Dr Campbell was my friend — my third grandpa. I had big plans about how we could make him well again when he came home from The Rowans, when spring came to Cloudberry.

Mum and Dad were so busy talking about who to tell and why Dr Campbell named us as his closest family that they didn't even talk about all the great things about him or how sad it was that he had died.

When we got back to Holly Cottage, I dumped my case in the hallway, ran straight up to my room and threw myself on my patchwork quilt. I wanted to be on my own while I got used to the idea that I wouldn't be able to see Dr Campbell ever again.

It would have been better if he had died in the castle, in his own home. But it was too late for that now. At first, I could hardly bear to look up to the lifeless castle. That picture of him sitting in the chair by his fire in the library was so comforting, and I wanted to remember him like that.

But when I finally dried my eyes, I felt as though a magnet was pulling me towards the castle. I found the courage to look up to it again. I suddenly wanted to visit Cloudberry Castle. It seemed to beckon me across towards it. I know it sounds mad, but it sometimes seems to me that buildings have personalities, and I don't like to hurt their feelings.

The castle was feeling lonely; I just knew it. I had to go over there.

I washed my face in the bathroom on the top landing and then I started to go downstairs. But I had another thought, and ran back up to my room. I had decided to take my ballet shoes with me.

When I got downstairs, I grabbed my jacket.

"Just going out on my bike for a bit. I'll check on Bella at the stables," I called into the kitchen, where Mum and Dad were chatting rather secretively at the table over their mugs of steaming tea.

"Don't be long, love," said Mum. "We've still got to chat to Dad about our adventure in London. He's made a lovely Sunday dinner for us."

"Okay, Mum," I replied.

As I was pulling on my wellies, I heard Mum talking to Dad.

"Really, Dan, I wish you hadn't told Katie the news about Dr Campbell in the car. She might think that every time she goes away, something sad is going to happen. You know how sensitive she is."

I didn't wait to hear Dad's answer. I guessed it would be something like: "You can't shelter them from bad news, Beth." Typical Dad. He believes in being honest with us, and I suppose I like that.

Even though the happy feeling I'd had after the ballet in London had gone away, I was glad that I knew the truth. I can always tell when my parents are telling fibs, or avoiding telling me things. They don't realise that nothing makes sense when they hide things from us.

There was no good time to tell me about Dr Campbell.

I jumped on my bike and slung my ballet shoes on the handlebars. I began to pedal really fast. I was desperate to get to the castle, but I checked in on Bella first. She neighed happily when she saw me and put her head out of the stable door to greet me. I changed her water and topped up the hay net, then kissed her goodbye and headed over to the castle.

As I drew nearer I heard a voice calling me — the voice of the castle, perhaps. *Ah, Katie. Katie Mackenzie. I thought you would come. What would I do without you?* said the voice.

I realised it wasn't the castle speaking to me. It was Dr Campbell! Maybe, just maybe, Dad had got mixed up or had been told the wrong news. There were so many old people at The Rowans. Maybe a different one had died? After all, it didn't make sense for the matron to call Dad — Mum said so. What if Dr Campbell was back in the castle, having made a brilliant recovery?

Or he could be lying inside in bed? Maybe he needed some medicine or something to eat? I *had* to get in there. His spirit was in there; I just knew it. I remembered a secret way into the castle that Sorcha and I had discovered last Christmas.

I ran through the courtyard, looking for the little door which you hardly notice if you don't know about it. It must have been for servants to use when the castle was first built in 1856. It's tucked into the rounded bit of one of the turrets, and you can't see it from the front of the castle. I ran to the back of the furthest turret and saw the curved door, with its flaking grey paint. I pushed it firmly. It opened easily. I didn't even feel spooked as I stepped inside. I just wanted to find out if there was anything more I could do to help Dr Campbell.

It was quite a sunny afternoon, which was just as well because I had no idea how to put on any of the lights. I found myself in the lowest part of the castle, where the old kitchens are. They haven't been used for years, as Dr Campbell used a tiny kitchen upstairs instead. There were some dusty copper pans hanging on a wall and an old bell system, which must have let the servants know where they were wanted upstairs: SITTING ROOM, MORNING ROOM, DRAWING ROOM, BALLROOM, LIBRARY, GALLERY, MASTER BEDROOM, DRESSING ROOM … it sounded like something from a game of Cluedo. But even that thought didn't frighten me.

Underneath the bells, there were little pigeon-hole shelves marked: BUTLER, COOK, LADY'S MAID, PARLOUR MAID, GROOM, FOOTMAN, HOUSEKEEPER. So many jobs to be done in a big castle. Yet Dr Campbell coped without staff. Mum and I were his only helpers. I gazed out to the cobbled courtyard and I could easily imagine the castle in the olden days, when it would have been buzzing with life, upstairs and downstairs. Fabulous feasts would have been prepared in these kitchens by rosy-cheeked cooks.

Mum said it used to be owned by the Thane of Lochvale and that many famous people had stopped off here on their way into the Highlands — even Queen Victoria and her family when it was snowing heavily once on the way to Balmoral, their castle on Deeside. There would have been horses and carriages arriving at the front steps, probably children playing in the gardens and parties galore, with girls dancing in pretty long dresses, trimmed with lace and flowers, to the sound of fiddles and pipes. I imagined that I could hear music playing and, with a skip in my step, I headed further into the castle to see what I would find.

6. The Secret Room

Dr Campbell lived on the floor above. I knew all about the castle because we were always allowed to run around wherever we liked when we came to visit. And I had been over plenty of times with Mum when she was taking jugs of vegetable broth and Dr Campbell's favourite snacks, like freshly baked sponge cakes and scones. I often made sweet treats for him too. He adored little squares of fudge and tablet, and sticky Florentines too. One time, I took over some New York brownies which Mum showed me how to make. He said brownies were "too American" for his taste but that he would try them anyway. Then he started to speak with an American accent, using words like "honey" and "baby" and "dime" and "dollar"! He said the brownies had turned him into an American.

I'm not sure how many times I had been in the castle,

but I spent so many hours thinking and dreaming about it that I seemed to know everything about it. Sometimes I would stand in my bedroom and look over to all the windows and try to work out which belonged to which room.

As I made my way up the servants' stairs, I thought that it must have been very expensive for one person to live in such a big house. Even in our tiny Holly Cottage, Mum was always saying that we had to be careful about wasting electricity and food and looking after the furniture. She said it is very expensive to replace things and that money doesn't grow on trees.

And I supposed it must have been really lonely too, living alone in the castle. Dr Campbell had made a little house inside the big house. It was sort of a flat, so he didn't have to heat up the whole castle.

When I reached the corridor leading to the library, I couldn't hear his voice talking to me any more, but I felt perfectly safe. Some people might have found it spooky, wandering around a huge castle all alone, but it's a kind castle because Dr Campbell was a kind man.

"Dr Campbell?" I called. "Are you there?"

Silence.

"Dr Campbell?"

This time, there was a creaking sound, as though someone was walking over floorboards. I convinced myself that he was walking towards me.

"Is that you, Dr Campbell?" I asked, tiptoeing along the corridor.

I saw his library ahead — the room I can see from my bedroom. *Please let him be in there!* I thought. I crept inside, half expecting to see him wandering around. The room was bright with sunlight. Maybe that's why he liked this room so much. There were ashes in the fireplace and an old cup of tea on a saucer by Dr Campbell's chair. For some silly reason, I felt the teacup to see if it was still warm. But it was freezing cold and the dregs of tea looked mouldy inside it. Of course Dr Campbell wasn't there.

It made me very sad to see the stick he poked the fire with hanging on a hook and a pair of slippers lying by his chair. His notebook and pen were on the little table. He obviously hadn't even taken them to The Rowans. I remembered he said he wouldn't write any more. I looked at the notebook, but it was completely empty. It must have been a brand new one he was about to start when he was taken away. How I longed to find out what was written in his notebooks!

I realised at that moment that he was gone forever. The voice I heard outside must have been in my head and my heart. A friendly voice which gave me the courage to come inside. I sat in his chair, which smelled of logs and heather honey. I felt some comfort and a lot of pain, all at once. The tears fell silently over my cheeks.

I looked over to Holly Cottage. You would never imagine that I could see into this room, because it's impossible to see into my room from Dr Campbell's library. No wonder he shook his head when I knew about the key for the secret cupboard. He must have found that very confusing. I suppose I had always assumed that if I could see someone, then they could see me back.

I noticed some photographs on the piano and went to look at them closely. Dr Campbell looked so young. And that must have been his wife next to him. There was a school picture of a girl and a boy — probably Dr Campbell's grandchildren because it looked like quite a modern picture.

I walked out to the corridor. There were closed doors on every side. I had never seen inside some of the rooms before. For the first time, I noticed a door which blended into the panelling. It was slightly open. I knew I should be getting home and probably shouldn't be nosy, but I was so intrigued to see what was inside.

I poked my head round the door of the room and gasped with surprise. It was a stunning ballroom, like the one in Cinderella!

7. The Swan Princess

The ballroom had three big, fancy chandeliers dangling from the ceiling, which was decorated with pretty white plasterwork — I think some of the patterns are of cloudberries and their dainty flowers. Large mirrors hung on the high walls and they made the room look even bigger. There were elegant chairs round the edges, with gold legs and powder-blue velvet seat-pads. But they were dusty and faded. It looked as though no one had been in this room for years and years. And yet … it had lots of feelings in it. Perhaps many happy parties had been held there.

Why have I never noticed this before? I wondered. I was looking at the castle with new eyes. *And why had the door been left ajar?* Deep inside I wondered if Dr Campbell had wanted me to find this room.

I sat on one of the blue velvet seats and put on my pink ballet shoes. I noticed an old-fashioned gramophone out of the corner of my eye, and went over to look at it. There was a pile of records by the side of it. I'd seen these sort of big discs before at Granny and Grandpa Mackenzie's in Edinburgh — "long-playing records", Grandpa called them.

I looked through them. Most were wartime songs, Scottish dance music or classical symphonies. Then I saw it. I could not believe my eyes: the music of *Swan Lake* by Pyotr Tchaikovsky! It was as if I was meant to find it.

Carefully, I slipped the disc out of the sleeve. It looked as if it was new. I placed it on the turntable and pressed START. The arm with the needle on it clicked its way over and lowered itself down towards the grooves on the record.

I felt as if I was back at Covent Garden. This time I was centre stage, dancing the part of Odette, just like Anya Swarovsky. I forgot about my sadness and confusion as I danced round the ballroom, practising my *pirouettes*, *pas de chat* and *jetés*. All of my energy poured out as I travelled round the room in full flight. Surely Mrs Miller would choose me as Odette. She *had* to. I knew that if I did my best I could dance the part better than the other girls.

I didn't want to stop and face real life, but my energy

came to an end as the music stopped, and I fell to the floor, completely exhausted. I have no idea how long I had been away from Holly Cottage, but I thought I'd better head back over there for Sunday dinner. I changed out of my ballet shoes and let myself out of the secret door, cycling back towards home. I could hear Mum calling through the trees.

"Katie, where are you? What are you doing? Katie!"

She sounded so worried that I felt very guilty. I guessed I would be in trouble.

"Coming, Mum!" I called.

Mum *was* very angry with me. I've never disappeared on the estate like that before. It covers hundreds of acres and it must have been worrying for Mum when she couldn't find me. You wouldn't know where to start searching for anyone at Cloudberry.

"Where on earth were you?" asked Mum once we were back in the kitchen. "I checked the stables three times."

"Just exploring. I was thinking about Dr Campbell," I said. I didn't tell her I'd been inside the castle. I had never lied to her before, but I knew she would make me promise never to go in there again, and I couldn't bear that. The castle kept Dr Campbell alive in my heart — and I knew that, with the ballroom to practise in, my dreams of becoming a ballerina might come true. It was going to be my secret.

We sat down for Sunday dinner in the kitchen.

"Thanks, Dad. This is lovely," I said, as we tucked into a wonderful roast dinner. Dad's potatoes are always super-crispy and he makes his golden Yorkshire puddings from scratch.

"Glad you like my humble offerings — after being in the big city," said Dad.

"Your roast tatties are always the best," I said.

"But I loved the chocolate cake at Edwards," piped up Sorcha.

"Well, I hope my dessert is just as good," said Dad.

"It smells wonderful," said Mum. The air was filled with the delicate aroma of warm chocolate and sweet pears.

"So, how was the ballet, girls?" asked Dad.

"I loved the tutus," said Sorcha.

"It was magical," I said. "One day it will be me on that stage."

"Well, if you keep practising, love, you never know what might happen," said Dad. "And I can't wait to see you in Mrs Miller's production, no matter what part you get."

"Yeah, I'm trying my best to impress her, but it's a shame I don't have more space for practising here. My room's so tiny," I said.

"Well, we'd all like a bigger house, but at least we've got each other, eh?" he smiled.

I nodded and tucked into a bowl of chocolate and pear crumble with extra crunchy oatmeal topping, served with homemade fudge ice cream. I'm so lucky that my mum and dad make such yummy meals. Dad certainly *had* been busy while we were away.

"You've got more ice cream than me!" said Hamish, peering into Sorcha's bowl.

"No, I have not," argued Sorcha. "You're just greedy!"

Hamish lashed out at this insult and smacked Sorcha's arm with his spoon. Very soon, a full fight had broken out, with Hamish pulling Sorcha's hair. Mum thought they both needed a late afternoon nap, so she took them upstairs to her and Dad's room and closed the curtains. I could hear her telling them stories and singing nursery rhymes, just like she used to do for me when I was trying to get off to sleep.

Dad and I started washing the dishes, and a few minutes later, Mum tiptoed back down. Once all the chores were done, the three of us sat in the family room on one of the velvet sofas, with the stove blazing and the little lamps on as darkness fell over Cloudberry. They had coffee and I had a mug of hot chocolate, and we nibbled on peppermint creams wrapped in shimmering emerald green foil.

"It's a terrible loss when a close friend dies," said Mum.

"I wish I had said more kind things to him the last time I saw him," I said.

"Oh, Katie!" said Mum. "No one has been kinder to Dr Campbell than you. He very much appreciated your sweetness. He told me so when we left The Rowans on Boxing Day."

"Did he really?" I said.

She nodded. "He adored you."

That was a very nice thought.

When I looked up at the castle that night, the stars were twinkling brightly over it, and it seemed as if they were winking at me.

8. Mallie Lennox

Over the next few weeks, spring flowers burst into life around our cottage, all the way up to the castle. More snowdrops appeared first of all, then bluebells, along with yellow daffodils and pink tulips. They looked like a beautiful carpet leading me from Holly Cottage up to the castle. The splash of colour made me feel a little more cheerful, after so many weeks of drab greys and browns. I usually made my way over to the castle once a week or so. I always told Mum I was going to see Bella, and I *did* check on her each time. It's just that I was also dancing round the ballroom! At ballet lessons, Mrs Miller was teaching us the steps required for *Swan Lake*, and I was practising them in Cloudberry Castle.

One Thursday after ballet class, when I was dancing the role of the Swan round the ballroom, I decided it was time to let my best friend Mallie in on the secret. It would be such fun to bring Mallie up to the ballroom. It could be our secret den, somewhere to dance our worries away and prepare for the auditions for the ballet production.

My mind was made up. I would find a way to get Mallie into the castle. I rushed back to Holly Cottage for tea. Mum was very busy cooking with Sorcha and Hamish, so I knew it wasn't the best time to ask.

After I did my homework, I set to work in my room. I decided to make *Swan Lake* tutus for Mallie and me. I found some white netting and fluffy swan's down in Mum's big sewing box. I searched through my cupboard and found two plain white leotards. Using Granny Mackenzie's old sewing machine, I stitched the netting round the waist and the swan's down round the neck. Lovely! They turned out beautifully. I hung them up at the back of my cupboard, along with two tiaras, decorated with down. Another secret. I was starting to like secrets.

"Mum," I said at breakfast the next morning. "Would it be okay if Mallie comes over tomorrow to hang out here?"

"I don't see why not, love," Mum replied. "Dad's not going out for lunch, for a change, so he'll be here and I don't have much planned, except for starting our spring clean of the cottage. So, yes, that would be lovely. She can stay overnight, if you like."

"Wow. Thanks, Mum. That would be great. I'll ask her at school today, and then you can call her Mum tonight to confirm times," I said.

"Actually, I'll see Moira Lennox at choir practice tonight, so I can sort it all out then." Mum smiled.

I was dying to ask Mallie if she wanted to come.

I like going to school in Lochvale. Our classroom for Primary 6 and 7 looks out over the village square. We are taught by Mr Matthews, who might be quite funny, but is *very* disorganised. We have to join up with other year groups, as there aren't that many children in the school. When we have whole school assembly on a Friday morning, there are only about sixty of us in the hall.

As we all filed into our usual seats that Friday, I spotted Mallie a little bit ahead of me. She's very small, with loads of red hair, gorgeous green eyes and sweet freckles. I caught up with her.

"Hey, Mallie," I whispered, "want to come over to my house tomorrow for a sleepover?"

"Brilliant. That sounds amazing!" Mallie smiled. "I've been getting really bored at weekends lately. There's nothing to do in winter. I can't wait."

"MALLIE LENNOX. BE QUIET UNLESS YOU WANT FRIDAY DETENTION. I'M GOING TO BE HERE UNTIL SIX O'CLOCK, SO I DON'T CARE!"

It was the headmistress, Mrs Jennings. She can really shout.

We didn't discuss the sleepover again until break when we chatted together in the queue for fruit. (Usually it's apple, banana or orange, apart from one legendary day when we had sweet, tender mango.)

"I'm so pleased you can come," I said. "And, Mallie, I'm going to tell you a massive secret tomorrow. In fact, I'm going to *show* it to you," I said.

"What is it? I will burst if you don't tell me," she complained.

"Wait and see. Bring your wellies — and your ballet shoes," I said.

"Ballet shoes sound good. But wellies? This better not be a prize cow or something. I will *not* be impressed if it's something farm related."

I laughed. Mallie lives on Tullyacre Farm on the far side of Cloudberry, and she has three farm-mad brothers, so she gets bored with things like tractors, sheep and crops. That's why she loves ballet so much. Her brothers say ballet is rubbish, but she doesn't care. Mallie says they are "muddy idiots".

"Don't worry, Mallie. You'll definitely like it. Trust me," I said. "The wellies are just to get us to the secret place."

"Okay, that sounds interesting. I'll bring my new CD player too. And I'll make some treats tonight for a midnight feast. Coconut ice and caramel shortcake. Yum-yum," said Mallie.

"Cool. My favourites! My mum will tell your mum all about it tonight at choir."

Mallie high-fived me. We were both really excited about the sleepover and Friday afternoon at school seemed to drag on forever. I don't know why we have to do comprehension on Friday afternoons. It was a passage about a parrot called Bill, with ten boring questions. We are all far too tired on Fridays for a big writing job like that. But Mr Matthews says we are better doing something hard that focuses the mind than something easy, otherwise we would all misbehave. I think he based this rule on the fact that when he arrived at Lochvale Primary, he let us play charades on the first Friday afternoon and we all went a bit crazy.

After school each day, I queue for the school bus and the driver drops me at the top of the road into the Cloudberry estate. I run down the road for about a quarter of a mile to Holly Cottage. It really helps Mum out if I get the bus, as she has to collect Sorcha and Hamish from school at lunchtime every day. Hamish is in the nursery, which is attached to Lochvale Primary, and Sorcha is in Class 1/2.

When I got in from school, Mum and Dad were very stressed. The atmosphere was tense. I tried to tell Mum that Mallie was definitely able to come for the sleepover, but she just nodded distractedly and carried on speaking to Dad — like she does when she's talking to him about money worries, or a mean child at school who's being nasty to one of us.

I picked up my copy of *Sugar* magazine and flopped on the pink sofa, trying to hear what they were saying, while reading an article called, *The Comeback for Kitten Heels*. Oh, how I wished I could go back to being like Sorcha and Hamish, who never seemed to notice anything strange going on with Mum and Dad, so long as they were fed and watered on time every day.

I couldn't understand what they were talking about at first.

"I'm actually surprised they didn't arrive sooner than this," said Mum.

"Yeah, but you know what they're like. They hardly made it up here when the old man was alive," said Dad. "I can't believe they didn't come to the funeral."

"But why do they want to talk to us?" said Mum.

"Probably just to ask some questions about their father. I assume they'll be selling the castle now, so there will be a lot to see to," said Dad. "Dr Campbell must have a great deal of paperwork. He once told me that he wrote a ground-breaking book years ago about the building of the Pyramids of Giza. Like the famous

Egyptologist, Howard Carter, he was one of the finest experts on ancient Egypt. He was on TV, and the book sold millions of copies in America. I think that was how he was able to buy the Cloudberry estate. But his family thought it was too cold and remote up here and never settled, apparently."

"I remember some of that," said Mum. "But I generally chatted to him about how to make the best stock for Scotch broth and stuff like that."

"We certainly had some good chats over Christmas drinks. He told me that he was born in Glasgow and thought of himself as Scottish, but his son prefers London life, as that's where he spent his childhood when the doctor was a lecturer in Egyptian archaeology at University College London," explained Dad.

"I can't help feeling uneasy about all this," Mum went on. "They will have to sort out the legal side of things, I'm sure. But how can we help? And what about our cottage? We don't even have any paperwork about the lease. Dr Campbell always said we didn't need a piece of paper between friends, but that hasn't left us in a strong position now, has it? Could they ask us to leave, Dan? I'm really scared."

I took a deep breath and ran up to my room. I didn't want to hear any more. I couldn't imagine what it would be like living anywhere except on the Cloudberry estate.

I had guessed by now that Dr Campbell's family must be staying up at the castle. At *my* castle.

9. The Campbells at the Castle

As soon as I got to my room, I looked out of my window. *Oh no!* I was right. There was a big car in front of the castle and the lights were on inside.

"Now I won't be able to take Mallie in there tomorrow!" I muttered to myself. There were so many things running through my head. What if they *did* throw us out of Holly Cottage? How long were they going to be here for? And would they really be selling the castle? What if someone horrid bought it? Our whole life seemed to be turned upside down.

I tried to see what was going on up at the castle. I thought that someone was taking things out of the car, but I couldn't get a proper view from my window, so I decided to take my bike out and have a better look.

"Just popping out, Mum," I called.

"Take Sorcha with you, please," said Mum. She and Dad obviously wanted some peace and quiet. Hamish was sitting quietly watching a DVD, which was very unusual.

"Okay," I replied. "Sorcha, you get in the trailer and I'll pull you along with the bike," I said. Mum wrapped us up in coats and scarves as it was still bitterly cold.

"What are we going to do, Katie?" asked Sorcha, as I cycled towards the castle.

"We're on a secret mission," I replied. "Just stay nice and quiet."

"Yippee. We're spies," said Sorcha happily.

I stopped between some trees. There were no leaves to hide us as there would be in summer, so I peeked out from behind a large tree trunk. Sorcha stood behind me, moving from one foot to another, trying to work out what we were supposed to be looking at.

"Let me see!" she said.

A girl of about fourteen was standing in front of the castle. She was very pretty, with blonde hair which was piled on her head like a bird's nest. She had lovely skin, all peaches and cream, and she looked very slim, but with a grown-up shape. Something about her looked vaguely familiar to me.

I know that girl from somewhere, I thought. Suddenly, it came to me.

I know! She's the girl in the photo on the piano. She was

obviously one of Dr Campbell's grandchildren.

A man came out to the big, black car. He was tall and thin, with dark hair, brushed back off his face.

"How long do we have to stay here for, Dad?" asked the girl. "It's so boring and the castle smells disgusting. Can we go home to London soon?"

I was insulted. How dare she talk about my beloved Cloudberry that way? She seemed so spoiled. Didn't she like being close to where her lovely Grandpa had lived?

"I don't know, Keira," said the man. "We might go in the morning, or we might stay until Sunday. It depends. The lawyers can't find any of Grandpa's papers and we're going to ask those people who live in Holly Cottage if they know where he might have kept them. If we don't find his instructions of what he wanted to do with the estate, then it will be ages before we can sell the castle. And the longer we have to wait, the longer it will be until we can buy that lovely new house in Kensington — the one you love, with the swimming pool and tennis court."

"She's so bratty!" said Sorcha.

I gasped in agreement. They just wanted Dr Campbell's cash! Why didn't they want to cherish his belongings and feel his spirit around them?

"Who are they?" whispered Sorcha.

"Dr Campbell's family," I explained.

"Are they making Mummy scared?" she asked.

"Yeah, I think so," I replied, astonished that Sorcha was more aware than I had imagined.

"Come on, Super Spy, we'd better get back. And Sorcha, this is our secret, okay?"

"Yeah. I love secrets," she said. "I'll hardly tell anyone."

I cycled back to the cottage. I didn't know whether to tell Mum and Dad about what I'd overheard. I decided they might be annoyed with me for taking Sorcha on a spying mission, so I kept quiet.

After tea, Mrs Renton from the post office arrived. That always means Mum and Dad are going out together. It hardly ever happens, but when they need a baby-sitter, Mrs Renton is our favourite. She always brings things from the post office, like rubber stamps, money boxes and notebooks, which Sorcha and I love to play with. We always set up our own post office on the kitchen table.

"Aren't you going to choir tonight, Mum?" I asked.

"No, sweetie. Dad and I are going to have a chat with the Campbell family up at the castle," Mum explained.

"Oh no. I wanted you to discuss everything about the sleepover with Mallie's mum tonight, remember?" I wailed. I felt a bit teary. It was all going wrong, and Mum hadn't even remembered about my plans with Mallie.

"Don't worry, Katie. I'll call Moira instead. Mallie can still come, darling."

"Okay, thanks," I said.

I went up to my room to see what was going on up at the castle now. There were more lights on than I had ever seen, and the Campbells were walking about the rooms, searching in cupboards and drawers. I was glad I'd tidied the ballroom for Mallie coming.

It made me so angry that all they wanted to do was get enough money to buy a fancy house in London. From what I'd seen of London, it was a very nice place to go to for a weekend, but I couldn't imagine living there forever. Keira didn't know anything about how much fun it was to live here at Cloudberry. There are such pretty things that happen all year round. Wildflowers decorate the grasses in spring, perfumed rose petals scent the summer days, amber cloudberries colour autumn, and in winter, the wonderland of Christmas is magical, with sparkle and snow. It's the best place in the whole world.

I wished I could go up there with Mum and Dad and find out what was going on. I wondered if I could sneak out and hide in the trees again, but if Mrs Renton noticed, she would get such a fright. And anyway, there probably wasn't much I'd be able to learn from outside the castle.

I put on my ballet music CD and tried out some moves in my room. But it felt so cramped compared with the ballroom. I was restless, so I tidied my room for Mallie coming the next day.

When I went downstairs for tea, Mrs Renton wanted me to play Hungry Hippos, but I said I had homework to do, and I took two slices of buttered toast and a glass of milk up to my room. I was too busy worrying to play childish games.

This time when I looked up to the castle, I could see my parents sitting down in the library. It was odd seeing my parents up there.

I think I'll go and get Dad's bird-watching binoculars, I decided.

When I came back from my parents' room, I held up the binoculars and had a good look at my parents' expressions. They seemed to look confused. Mum was shaking her head a lot. It didn't look like a very happy discussion. Then they left the room and soon I saw them walking down the road towards Holly Cottage.

Within a few minutes, I heard the front door go and I rushed to the top of the stairs. I sat silently as they chatted to Mrs Renton, hardly daring to breathe.

All I heard at first was Mum talking.

"They can't find a certain box. The letter of wishes from Dr Campbell, left at The Rowans, says everything to do with his estate is in a wooden box in a secret cupboard, but no one knows where this cupboard is. We certainly don't. It's so embarrassing that he's named us as his next of kin! The family must be terribly hurt, but what can we do?"

"Well, it's just what they deserve," said Mrs Renton. "He named you because he trusted you, love. You did so much for him, Beth. I really shouldn't disclose professional information, but I never saw a single card or letter coming in for him with a London postmark. And as far as I know, they hardly ever visited here either. He often came in with envelopes for recorded delivery. He said they were cheques to help the family out. He was such a kind man. I don't know what went wrong between him and his family. Maybe he was just too far away and they forgot about him with their busy lives." I thought about Granny and Grandpa Berry coming to see us regularly all the way from Boston. Families usually did that sort of thing, as far as I knew.

As I was thinking about what Mrs Renton said, I suddenly had a thought about where the box might be. In the secret cupboard I used to see Dr Campbell locking up when he finished his writing. The one we joked about at The Rowans.

I went into my room and lay on my bed, thinking about it.

Should I tell Mum about the chat I had with Dr Campbell? I wondered. Maybe I could help his family out, and in a way that would be like helping the doctor. If I led them to the box, they would see how kind people who live at Cloudberry are. And on a selfish note, I must admit, I thought it might also mean that they'd be gone by tomorrow, so that Mallie and I could dance in the ballroom as planned.

I realised I had to tell Mum and Dad what I knew. I flew downstairs at top speed. Not very balletic at all.

"Mum, I think I know where the box is," I said.

"What? What are you talking about, Katie?" asked Mum, looking very confused.

"Dr Campbell's box of paperwork? He mentioned something to me — at The Rowans. Can I show you all? Will you take me up to the castle? Please?" I asked.

"Katie, are you sure about this?" said Mum.

"I don't know. But I remember it clearly. There's a secret cupboard."

"Come on then, but you had better be sure, or this could be very embarrassing. And please tell us everything you know, otherwise it might look like we've been keeping secrets from the Campbells," she said.

"Okay, I'll explain everything on the way up there," I promised.

"I'll leave this to you, Beth," said Dad. "My legs are aching and I could do with a nice chilled glass of white wine in front of the telly."

10. The Box of Wishes

Mum knocked politely on the big, black door at the front of the castle, even though she had her own keys from when she took food in for Dr Campbell.

"I'm so sorry to disturb you, David," she said to Dr Campbell's son. "This might sound a bit mad, but my daughter Katie thinks she might know where your father kept his papers."

"Oh? Really?" he said, peering over his spectacles. "You had better come in." He looked nothing like Dr Campbell — his features were much sharper and lizard-like.

I went into the library nervously. David's wife, Mariella, was working at the antique desk with a shredding machine. She was very tall and thin, with blonde highlights and a suntan. It looked as if she was shredding lots of letters and cards to pieces. Their daughter, Keira, was lying on a sofa, reading *Closer* magazine. She didn't sit up. I smiled and went straight to the hidden door at the side of the fireplace. Anyone would think it was part of the wooden panelling on the walls.

"This is it here," I announced, feeling very proud of myself. "The secret cupboard he told me about."

I could hear everyone gasp with surprise as I reached behind the clock on the mantelpiece for the key, just as I had seen Dr Campbell do so many times before.

"Katie," said Mum. "Have you done this before?"

"No, but I've seen Dr Campbell doing it lots of times. When the lights are on in winter and I'm practising ballet at my barre in my room, I can see ... *could* see Dr Campbell sitting on his chair writing by the fire, and then he would lock the notebooks away in this cupboard. Then he mentioned it to me at The Rowans on Boxing Day."

"Brilliant," said David. "I would never have noticed the cupboard. Good girl!" He smiled.

I was so proud that I was helping Dr Campbell's family. I thought it would be lovely if Keira and I could be friends. She looked very glamorous close-up. She wore loads of black eyeliner and cool denim shorts, with thick tights underneath.

I fumbled around with the key nervously. It was the first time in my life that adults have relied on me to solve a problem, and I felt all the eyes in the room on my back.

David, Mariella, Keira and Mum.

As I pulled the unlocked door towards me, David stood right behind me.

"My God. She's a genius. There's a box in there all right!" he cried.

I noticed there was a pile of notebooks too, but Mum and I felt rather awkward after the box was found. It wasn't right for us to wait and see what was inside it, no matter how curious we were.

"Well done, Katie, darling!" said Mum. She turned to the family. "We'll get going now, but if we can be of any more help, you know where we are."

"We can't thank you enough," said David. "Let's hope this contains all the information we need to move things on."

"I hope so. See you around," said Mum. "Perhaps you would be kind enough to firm up our lease agreement for Holly Cottage as soon as possible."

David nodded, but was preoccupied with the box already, as were Keira and Mariella.

"Bye, everyone," I said. Much to my disappointment, Keira and Mariella barely looked over. And with that, we were shown to the front door by David, and we left the castle.

"Wow, Katie. There's a lot more going on in your mind than I know about, isn't there?" said Mum.

I nodded. "Maybe I'm a bit more grown up than you realise," I said.

"Yeah, maybe you are," said Mum, a little sadly. "I think I spend too much time concentrating on the wee ones."

"I don't mind that," I said. Then, feeling bolder, I asked, "Are you worried we might lose the cottage?"

"You know, the thing I'm really curious about is that it's so unlike Dr Campbell to leave us in a risky position with our lease. I wonder if he covers it at all in his last wishes. I can't believe he would leave us high and dry."

"Nor can I," I said.

She took my hand and we walked silently back to Holly Cottage, lost in our thoughts.

I didn't sleep well that night. Sometimes I get silly ideas in my head. I thought there was a witch looking in at my window. I got up to pull my curtains together properly, so there was no gap in the middle.

A while after that, I heard a noise. *What's that?* I thought. I was sure it was the tyres of a car crunching on the road from the castle. I froze as the noise stopped suddenly. The front door of our house seemed to rattle. Then I heard the car sound again, until it faded away in the distance.

I *had* to get up and see what was going on. I was feeling very spooked. I peeked out of my bedroom curtains bravely, but I couldn't see much at all. The castle was in total darkness. Nervously, I crept downstairs with my torch. I didn't want to wake up Mum and Dad. When I shone the torch at the front door, I realised that there was an envelope lying on the hall floor. Someone had put it through the letterbox — in the middle of the night. How odd. The clock in the kitchen said three o'clock. Who goes around delivering letters at that time?

I bent down to pick up the envelope. I was hoping it would not be sealed. I sat at the kitchen table and looked at it carefully with the help of the torch. It said, *To The Mackenzies* on the front.

I turned it over. The flap was just tucked in, not stuck down. It was so tempting, but would it be right for me to read it before Mum and Dad? What if there was something terrifying inside? I suppose I guessed who'd sent it, but I had no idea what it would contain.

With a trembling hand, I opened the envelope and pulled out the letter.

Cloudberry Castle,
February 20th

Dear Mr and Mrs Mackenzie,

We have now opened the box located by your daughter Katie. We are appalled and dismayed to learn of the way you have clearly influenced my late father, Dr Edmund Campbell.

No wonder you knew the whereabouts of the box: you have obviously discussed private matters regularly with him.

We will take up matters concerning the will with our lawyers in London, and we suggest you do what your conscience tells you is right.

Cloudberry belongs to us, and we will not rest until justice prevails.

It says in the box that a local lawyer by the name of Wilson is acting on my father's wishes, so you should contact him to make sure that you reverse what you have persuaded my father to do.

The castle is not rightfully yours and you cannot take it from us in this manner.

Devious people like you disgust me and make me despair about humanity.

Yours in disbelief,
David Campbell

I felt my throat going tight with panic. As I had suspected, the car must have been the Campbells leaving Cloudberry. Whatever they had found in the box clearly was not to their liking. Was it possible that Dr Campbell didn't want them to inherit the castle?

11. Tutus for Two

What did he mean by saying that "Cloudberry belongs to us"? Of course it belonged to them! I was very upset and confused, and yet I could not bear to worry my parents with the letter in the middle of the night.

I also had Mallie to think about. She was arriving in the morning, and I wasn't going to be much fun if I hadn't been to sleep at all.

I put the letter back in the envelope and laid it back on the hall floor where I found it. Quietly, I made my way back upstairs. I no longer felt that a witch was looking in, and I snuggled under my patchwork quilt. I couldn't quite understand what David Campbell was talking about and as exhaustion took over, I finally dozed off.

"Katie? Katie, wake up. Mallie will be here soon."

Dad was calling from the landing. It's hard for him to get up to my room, so he usually just shouts instructions up to me.

"Coming, Dad," I called, rubbing my eyes. I was curious to see if the letter had been lifted. I ran to the bathroom and peered over the banister. The envelope had gone. Mum and Dad must have read it by now.

We had scrambled eggs for breakfast, made by Dad. Very fluffy and delicious, on crunchy brown toast, rich with nuts and seeds. Sorcha and Hamish tucked in hungrily, chatting about exactly how chickens laid eggs, but there was no sign of Mum.

"Looks like the Campbells have left already," said Dad casually.

"Have they? That wasn't a very long stay," I replied.

"They've made Mummy cry," said Sorcha.

I looked at Dad.

"Och, it's just a silly letter they've sent," said Dad. "They've been adding two and two and getting five, it seems. As soon as we visit Mr Wilson, the lawyer, on Monday morning, we'll get the whole thing sorted out."

I had a shower to wake me up, and Mallie arrived with her mum about half an hour later. Mum appeared to greet our guests, looking tired. She was chatty enough while Mallie's mum, Moira, talked her through all of Mallie's little quirks. Why do mums talk as if we're invisible?

"Mallie tends to get tummy pains if she eats too much sugar," revealed Moira. "And she's got a tin full of tray-bakes, so you might want to ration those."

"Okay," said Mum. "Will do."

"She'll claim that she doesn't like vegetables, but she does ..."

Moira went on like this for ages, as if we were going to have Mallie to stay for months, as a refugee during a war or something. We went up to my room to listen to music.

Mallie looked out of the window up to the castle.

"Wow. I'd forgotten about this view of Cloudberry. It's amazing. Just like from a fairy tale."

I thought about that for a minute. I supposed she was right. Even fairy tales have nasty characters — but the good ones always triumph in the end.

"Can't you see the castle from Tullyacre?" I asked.

"No, we're round the bend in the river," she explained.

I was trying to work out how risky it would be to take Mallie into the castle. I had promised her a secret, but what if the Campbells *hadn't* gone back to London? Maybe they'd gone off on a visit, or in search of a lawyer, and would arrive back at any time. I wished I hadn't asked Mallie over after all. Imagine if they found me and my friend dancing in the ballroom? They seemed to think we already knew too much about Dr Campbell and his business. They would be really angry to see us using the castle as if we owned it. And yet, I didn't want to let Mallie down.

"See, I've brought everything you told me to," she said, emptying her bag out on my bed.

"Great," I smiled.

"I can't wait for the secret," she said.

"Me too," I agreed. "Look what I've made for us."

I opened my cupboard. "Ta-da!" I said.

Mallie looked at the swan tutus hanging on the rail.

"Wow. I love them!" she gasped.

"I thought you would," I said. "We're going to need those for the secret."

"Awesome. I thought they *were* the secret," said Mallie.

Just at that moment, Mum came up to my room with the blow-up bed and sleeping bag. I closed the cupboard door hurriedly.

"Well, girls, what are your plans?" she asked, making a big effort to sound cheery.

"We might take a couple of bikes around the estate and check on Bella, if that's okay?" I suggested.

"Sure, so long as you don't go too far and you stay together. I'll make lunch for twelve thirty, so make sure you're back for then. I was going to do some spring cleaning today, but I'm feeling lazy," said Mum, heading downstairs.

We packed our ballet shoes and the *Swan Lake* tutus

carefully in our ballet cases. Downstairs in the family room, Mum and Dad were building a LEGO city with Hamish and Sorcha. Mallie and I went into the kitchen, where we took a little picnic of things from the fridge. We put on our wellies and took mine and Mum's bikes from the shed.

"Follow me!" I called to Mallie. It was very dangerous, but a promise is a promise. We were going into the castle.

12. Hide and Seek

First, we went to see Bella at the stables.

"She's so cute," said Mallie, rubbing the little pony's white blaze.

"Yeah. Bless her little heart, she's always so pleased to see me," I said.

"Is this the secret then? Bella?" asked Mallie. "Are we going to put on our ballet shoes and do a dance for her?"

"Nope," I giggled. "We've just got to feed her, give her a quick brush down, change her straw and hay, then I'll reveal the secret."

"Cool," said Mallie, helping me to groom Bella.

"Let's go," I said once all our pony chores were done.

We cycled over towards the castle.

"We'll hide our bikes amongst the trees here," I said.

"Where are we going now?" asked Mallie.

"Inside the castle," I revealed.

"Really? Wow!" breathed Mallie. "Who does it belong to?"

I thought about the words of the letter that David Campbell had written. *Cloudberry should belong to us ...* Something was telling me that it didn't belong to them in the eyes of Dr Campbell.

"It doesn't really belong to anyone, since Dr Campbell died," I said.

"Are we allowed?" she asked.

"Mallie, are you up for it?" I said, avoiding answering her question.

"Yes. Definitely," she said.

"Well, that's all that matters." I smiled. "Come on, there's a secret door."

My fears started to fade as I felt close to Dr Campbell again. I never ever feel nervous in the castle. I was a little worried that the Campbells might have locked up the little door, but it was still unlocked.

I pushed it and entered, with Mallie following on.

"Just wait until you see this." I was so excited that I practically ran upstairs towards the ballroom.

"Slow down," called Mallie. "There's so much I'd like to look at."

"Sorry, Mallie. We can explore afterwards. I want you to see the best first."

I stopped to catch my breath outside the ballroom door.

"Here it is," I said, pushing the door open. "Our secret dance studio!"

I showed Mallie in.

She was silent. Lost in her thoughts. She walked around the room, touching the velvet of the chairs, and looking up at the sparkle of the chandeliers.

"Oh, Katie," she said. "This is from Cinderella!"

"I know. Isn't it wonderful? I just know my ballet can get better and better if I have a space like this to practise in. I'm sure I'll be good enough for Covent Garden one day."

We sat down and put on our ballet shoes and our white swan leotards. Mallie shivered.

"I know, it's freezing, but once we start dancing, we won't feel the cold," I said.

I went over to the gramophone and pressed START. The needle moved onto the Tchaikovsky record. It burst into life. Act 1. I recognised the music from Covent Garden — the woodwind, brass, percussion and strings.

"It's the music from *Swan Lake*," I said. "Let's do the steps Mrs Miller has been teaching us."

We danced round the room, practising *arabesques, battements frappés* and *fouettés en tournant* from all four acts. We covered the coming of age party at the beginning of the story, the scene by the lake when Odette reveals her curse by Baron Von Rothbart, the confusion when the sorcerer's daughter Odile acts as Odette, and the final death of the Swan Princess.

"Let's do the dance of the cygnets now," I said. "We link arms and do sixteen *pas de chat*. Come on."

Mallie was very excited. "This is magical," she breathed. "It's the best secret ever. I so hope we get good parts in *Swan Lake*. Can you imagine it? In Perth Theatre."

I nodded. If I didn't get to be Odette, then I hoped it would be Mallie.

"It's not long until the auditions," I said. "Maybe if we practise really hard, one of us will be lucky."

We must have danced for at least an hour. We didn't feel cold or tired. But the music came to an end and we eventually flopped on the floor, side by side, gazing up at the beautiful ceiling.

"If only we could go to ballet school instead of boring normal school," said Mallie.

"I would love that," I agreed. "But I would hate to live away from my family. I would miss them too much. Boarding school sounds mean. Like in *Jane Eyre*."

"Yeah," agreed Mallie. "I might hate my brothers, but I'd rather live with them than with strangers. Can we have our picnic? I'm starving."

"Yeah, I'll just get it," I replied. We ate the crisps, apples and grapes hungrily, and drank the fruit juice. We were just enjoying a slice of banana bread each when we heard a noise, which sounded very like the front door opening.

"Oh no!" I said. "That might be the Campbells back. We'll have to hide. Quick!"

"I thought it was okay to be in here," said Mallie. "I'm scared."

"Don't worry," I told her. "There are lots of places we can hide."

We grabbed our stuff and put off the lights in the ballroom, hovering by the door while we worked out what was going on.

"Can you hear anything now?" I asked Mallie.

"No. Let's get out into the corridor and see if we can see a car," she suggested.

We tiptoed out into the corridor and closed the door behind us. I ran to one of the big windows which overlooks the front of the castle.

"There's no car," I said. "How strange. We definitely heard a door creak open, didn't we?"

Mallie nodded. "Please just get us out of here," she begged.

"Yes, don't panic. I know some secret ways out. Follow me."

As we neared the set of stairs which lead down to the kitchens, we heard voices. It sounded as if there were small children there too. The voices weren't clear, but they were getting nearer.

"We'd better go in this cupboard," I said, remembering a deep linen cupboard from a Christmas game of hide and seek.

We stood silently in the cupboard with the lights off, so we were in complete darkness, which seemed to help us focus on the voices.

I couldn't believe my ears. It was Mum and Dad, with Sorcha and Hamish. Their voices were quite clear now.

"You honestly think he means for us to have the castle?" Mum was saying.

"I don't know what else to think," said Dad. "That's what the letter implies, doesn't it? And isn't it odd that Dr Campbell made sure that Katie knew about the secret cupboard? As if he wanted to be totally sure that our family knew more than his."

"I understand the logic of what you're saying, but I simply can't take it in," said Mum. "Us? Owning a vast fairy-tale castle? It's too incredible."

Mallie pinched me. "You own it," she breathed.

I didn't reply. Even though I'd read the letter, I was still shocked.

"Yes, it's weird," Dad went on. "I'm sure the family

will find a legal loophole to get their rightful inheritance
— and I really hope that happens — but in the meantime,
we will have to respect Dr Campbell's last wishes."

"Let's see what Mr Wilson says on Tuesday," said Mum.

They were wandering around, and their voices
eventually began to fade.

We stayed in the cupboard for another few minutes,
then peeked out of the door to see if the coast was clear.

"They've gone," I said. "Come and see the rest of the
place."

"Well, if you own it, then why not?" agreed Mallie.

We investigated the whole castle, including a lookout
room at the top of one of the turrets.

"It's just like being princesses!" said Mallie.

"Swan princesses," I said.

We finally left the castle and cycled round Lily's Lake,
before heading back to Holly Cottage in time for lunch.

The meal was laid out. Mum and Dad were doing the
crossword in the newspaper. Sorcha and Hamish were
hurtling down the stairs inside Mallie's sleeping bag.

"It's a two-man bobsleigh!" shrieked Hamish.

I rolled my eyes at Mallie. Why are boys so noisy?

"Bella is absolutely fine," I reported cheerfully to
Mum.

"That's good, sweetie," she said. She still looked tired
but gave us a lovely lunch, just like a French picnic.

There was crusty bread, with pale, creamy butter, brie cheese, grapes, salad, ham, salami and olives. Dessert was a home-made chocolate cake with lashings of white chocolate icing.

"That was fantastic, thanks, Mrs Mackenzie," said Mallie.

Hamish, Sorcha and Mum snuggled down for quiet time, while Mallie and I discussed our adventure in the privacy of my room.

"Wouldn't the castle be a wonderful ballet school?" Mallie said out of the blue.

Mallie had obviously read my mind.

13. Castle of Dreams

It was at four p.m. on Tuesday the 24th of February that Mr Wilson, the local lawyer from Lochvale, came to see us. He's a small man, with short, wiry hair and dark eyes, with an honest gaze.

Mum and Dad sat round the kitchen table as Dr Campbell's trusted lawyer prepared to read out the instructions. Sorcha and Hamish were playing happily in the garden. I was reading by the stove. I half expected to be asked to leave the room, but that did not happen.

Mr Wilson cleared his throat.

"Here are the words of Dr Edmund Campbell, written last August:

I am of sound mind and body, and it is my wish that the Mackenzie family of Holly Cottage, Cloudberry Estate,

Lochvale, Perthshire, namely Mr Daniel Mackenzie, and Mrs Elizabeth Mackenzie, and their three children, should become the rightful owners of my historic castle. All of my worldly goods within it shall also be theirs, along with the assets of the entire estate. I bequeath this to them due to the selfless and kindest care they have shown me over the last few years. I know they will not expect this, which is exactly why they deserve it. It is my hope that they will live in the castle and enjoy it in the way it deserves.

To my son, David, daughter-in-law, Mariella, and grandchildren, Keira and Dylan, I leave the sum of £5000 each, which should be taken from the savings bank account at the Royal Bank of Scotland, Lochvale."

"Oh my god," said Dad. In fact he kept on saying it. "The castle is definitely ours now, Beth."

Mum held her head in her hands and sobbed.

"Is it true, Mr Wilson?" she asked.

"Yes, Beth. It's a legally binding document, and unless the Campbells can prove that Dr Campbell was forced to sign this, or suffering from insanity, they will not be able to overturn this will," he replied.

"And can they prove either of those things?" asked Dad.

"Well, I was a witness when he signed it, along with two other legal partners, so that's not a line they can follow, and as for his mental health? He thought of that angle. His doctor wrote him a clean bill of mental health before he signed it. The Campbells will just have to get used to the fact that he hasn't done the conventional thing," explained Mr Wilson with a shrug of his shoulders.

Mum and Dad looked pained. I could not understand their reaction. Why were my parents not delighted with the news? I went over to the table.

"Can you explain some of this to me, please?" I said quietly. "I'm just left to pick up bits and pieces of what you're saying. I'm so confused. Why are we not pleased about this?"

"Sorry, Katie," said Mum. "It's so kind of Dr Campbell. But it isn't right. He's punishing his family through us. I don't want to own a castle if I'm not entitled to it. On the other hand, if we sell it, we will be richer than I could ever have imagined. I'm confused as well, darling."

"If you would permit me to interrupt you there, Beth," said Mr Wilson. "On the first count, you *are* entitled to it, as it was the heartfelt wish of the owner, and secondly, it might be harder than you think to sell it at the moment. Not many people can afford such a project and the banks aren't backing this kind of thing. Of course, it is a wonderful asset, if you hold on to it. That's what I would advise."

"That's out of the question, I'm afraid," said Dad. "There's nothing we can do with it. I'd like to sell it as soon as possible."

I stared at him. Dad was always spoiling my dreams. I did not even dare to voice my thoughts, but I felt annoyed with Dad. He didn't like ballet, he didn't want the castle, he was always too tired to play with us. I felt guilty immediately. Poor Dad. He would never know how it felt to dance around a ballroom at top speed. I knew I shouldn't blame him. But both Mum and Dad were ignoring the part of Dr Campbell's instructions where he said he hoped we would live in the castle. Surely we had to respect that wish?

14. The Ballet-school Book

Our life at Holly Cottage changed dramatically after that Tuesday. Mum and Dad were constantly talking about the castle and there was a sort of buzz of excitement and expectation in the air. We had gone from a completely predictable way of life to a state of constant change. But the one thing that didn't change for me was my obsession with ballet. The auditions for *Swan Lake* could not come quickly enough.

I still desperately wanted to dance Odette, but school life trudged along in between ballet classes. One Monday morning in class, just three days before the *Swan Lake* auditions, Mr Matthews allowed Mallie and me to go to the library to research our project on the American War of Independence.

We browsed through the shelves marked "American History".

"Here's a book on the Boston Tea Party," I said. "Mr Matthews mentioned that. Wasn't that when the people of Boston rebelled against the British government by tossing all the tea into the harbour? My Granny Berry told me all about it once. She comes from Boston, so does Mum."

"Great. You have insider info," said Mallie. "Let's take it over to the beanbags and have a flick."

We looked through the book and started to understand it more.

"They probably call it a 'tea party' to make it sound more fun," said Mallie.

"Yeah, exactly. How childish were they, wasting all that tea in a tantrum?" I added.

Gradually we lost interest in tea, and our thoughts turned back to ballet.

"Been practising in the ballroom lately?" asked Mallie.

"Yeah. I just hope all my extra work pays off," I said.

"Katie, you are by far the best dancer in the class. I'm sure that Mrs Miller will pick you as the Swan Princess," she replied.

"I'm not so sure," I said. "I wish I could discuss it with Mum, and have her watch me over at the ballroom and give me advice, but I can't tell her about the secret studio. If she bans me from going, I'd have nowhere to practise the big dance moves."

"She *might* understand," said Mallie. "After all, she

adores ballet too, and they do own the castle. My mum says it's definite now."

"Yeah, but my parents haven't exactly accepted it," I explained. "She and Dad are going to sell the castle as soon as they possibly can. To be honest, I think it's mainly Dad who wants rid of it. We don't act as if we own it."

Mallie shook her head sadly. "Who would sell a castle like that?" she said. I agreed with her. It was crazy.

"Hopefully no one will want to buy it," I said.

The librarian shooshed us, so we checked out our books, heading back to class as slowly as possible.

Everyone in the ballet class was jangling with nerves at the Thursday auditions in the church hall. There was a list of our names on the noticeboard, in the order we would be called forward to dance. I was second to last.

That's a really bad position! I thought. Mrs Miller would be tired by then, and the very last dance would probably stick in her mind more than the second to last.

But I knew I had to stay calm and do my best. I would look bratty if I asked to dance in a different order. Mum always says I should never act like a prima donna — vain and full of my own importance. She says working with a ballet troupe is about teamwork.

We all sat on a bench outside the main hall while we

waited for our turn. Mallie went long before me. I peeked in through the glass panels in the door as she danced. She was wonderful! So wistful and elegant.

"Well done, Mal," I said when she came out. "You were awesome. Are you going home now?"

"Are you kidding?" she asked. "I'm waiting for you, of course."

I smiled. "Tell me exactly what you had to do in there."

"Some warm-ups, then some steps from Act 1V — *arabesques, jetés, pliés ...*" she explained breathlessly.

At long last, my name was called. I went in and looked at myself in the long mirror. I was wearing my pink leotard, crossover cardigan and my second best ballet shoes. My hair was in a really good bun. Mrs Miller smiled. Her friend, Madame Lacomb was next to her. She is a very old lady who used to teach ballet in the village before Mrs Miller.

"Katie, we will begin by limbering up with some general steps," she announced. "Could you let us see a *demi-plié ... battement tendu ... rond de jambe à terre ... glissade ... saute ... arabesque ...*"

I did all that she asked of me, but I was dying for her to put on the music and ask me to dance Odette. Mrs Miller and Madame Lacomb were writing things down in their notebooks as I performed the warm-up steps.

I stood in first position while I waited for the next instruction.

"That will be all, thank you, Katie," said Mrs Miller.

I was shocked. *She hasn't asked me to dance properly yet,* I thought. *They must have already picked the main parts from the other auditions. All of that extra practising, and deceiving my Mum — for nothing.*

I did not dare question her, so I walked out of the room as gracefully as I could, feeling absolutely devastated inside.

As I pushed the door, Mrs Miller called me back.

"Katie, do come back. What a lovely display of self-discipline and control. I know you want to dance more, but you take instruction very well," she said. "We need that sort of obedience in our principal ballerinas. Of course we would like you to perform the part of Odette for us today. You may interpret the part to the music."

I smiled and took a deep breath. This was my favourite bit — proper dancing. When the music started, my body took over and I cannot remember anything that happened. I just danced with all my heart, as if I was in the ballroom at Cloudberry. The music ended and I came to a halt, although my brain was still dancing on.

"Well done, Katie. That was really lovely," she said. I wondered if she had said that to everyone. I guessed she had, as she was always very kind.

As I left the hall, I heard Madame Lacomb say, "Exceptional talent."

Mallie was waiting for me. "You were incredible," she said, hugging me. "If you don't get the lead part, then I'll faint from shock," she said.

"Oh, Mallie. Thanks. I used to be believe in happy endings, but now I'm not so sure."

It was a long week while we were waited for Mrs Miller's decision. I kept thinking that I could have done better at the audition.

"Don't worry, darling," said Mum when she saw me fretting at tea one night. "You did your best. Now you just have to hope."

"It's only a hobby, love," said Dad. "You act like your whole life depends on it!"

I didn't reply. Dad would never understand how I felt about ballet, so there was no point trying to explain it to him.

When we went back to ballet the next Thursday, there were rumours flying around the dance class.

"Did you know that Mrs Miller hasn't picked the parts yet as no one was good enough?" said know-it-all Alice Marks from Dunkeld.

"Well, I heard she wants the daintiest girl for Odette," said Emma Lambert.

I closed off my ears. I wasn't the daintiest. Milly Lawson is very petite, as is Mallie. The suspense was unbearable.

15. Odette, A Good Fairy

We went into the hall and I tried to work out what sort of mood Mrs Miller was in.

She began the process of putting us out of our misery.

"Girls, there is just one month to go before the show, and you all know all the parts already, so it has been hard for me to choose between dancers on this occasion. But the time has come for each of you to specialise in one role each. I have indeed decided on parts, and I thought the best thing was to print a list of names with parts against them."

I saw a huge bundle of papers in her hands. I felt panicky.

Mrs Miller prolonged the stress by carrying on: "I hope you will accept my decisions as final. You all danced beautifully at the auditions. I am proud of you all. We will not include most of the male roles in our production, but I will dance the part of Baron Von Rothbart, the evil sorcerer."

She handed out the sheets face down, but said we may not turn them over until she said so.

I was in anguish. *How much longer will this suffering go on?* I thought.

"You may turn over … NOW!" she announced.

My eyes danced over the page.

The Sovereign Princess	Mallie Lennox
Baron Von Rothbart	Mrs Miller
Odette, a good fairy	Katie Mackenzie
Odile	Alice Marks
The Baroness	Helen Hooper
Ladies of the court	Anna Blair
	Isla Stewart
	Iona Prentice
Swans	Molly Farquhar
	Jane Bruce
	Rachel Mather
	Abi Burns
	Fiona Aitken
Villagers, cygnets and servants	All other dancers

Joy of joys, I was chosen to dance the part of Odette in the big production! It was a dream come true. And Sorcha would be a cygnet.

"Congratulations, Katie," said most of the girls.

"Should have known the girl with the castle would get to dance the princess," said Fiona Aitken. I ignored her.

"I'm sure it's because of all my extra practising," I told Mallie, hugging her.

"Yeah, that and the fact you're naturally brilliant," she said. "You totally deserve it."

But a few people definitely thought I had been picked for the main role just because we were now the owners of the big castle on the hill.

Everyone in the village and at school had changed the way they treated us recently, which I thought was very silly. After all, we hadn't changed in any way. They acted as if we had won the lottery. Some were jealous and thought we were "posh" now, while others sucked up to us. It let me see that Dr Campbell could have got very hoighty-toighty in the village if he had wanted to, but he just wasn't that sort of person. And neither are we.

Mum was ecstatic with my news when she came to pick up me and Sorcha.

"Pleased you're a cygnet?" I asked my little sister on the way home in the car.

"Yeah, and I'm pleased you're Odette. I want to be as

99

good as you one day, Katie," she said.

"You'll be even better," I said. "Want me to try your hair up in a bun when we get home?"

"Yes please," she beamed.

When we got back home, she came up to my room and sat at my dressing table. I caught sight of her face in the mirror. She looked a little sad.

"What's wrong?" I asked.

"Katie, everyone says we're rich now, but I don't feel any richer. Do you?"

"Not at all. We're not richer. We're still the same, but we happen to own a castle now," I said as I piled her hair up with grips.

"It's a bit like a fairy tale," she said. "But I don't want us to change."

"We won't, I promise," I said. "Now, how's that?" I pinned the final grip in place.

"Lovely," she said. "Can I have it like this on the day of the show?"

"Course you can. Anything for a lovely little cygnet."

All of our grandparents were very excited by the news that we now owned the castle. They decided to come for a weekend at the beginning of April, and chat to Mum and Dad about what they should do with it. Dad said the castle was a "mixed blessing". It was valuable, yet falling to pieces.

I hoped with all my heart that my grandparents would see the fun side of living in a castle and pass that idea on to my parents. Now that one of my ballet dreams had come true, another was starting to take shape in my mind. I was sure that Granny Berry would understand. I was dying to see her again, and I had loads of questions about the Boston Tea Party to ask her for my project.

The Cloudberry estate was looking very pretty when our grandparents were due to arrive. Lots of flowers had come out and the colours were gorgeous — lots of whites and shades of pink and purple. The trees had new leaves, and the blossom trees which line the driveway were all bursting into delicate bloom.

It was a Friday afternoon and Hamish and Sorcha were playing at knights and princesses in the front garden, keeping watch for the arrival of Grandpa Mackenzie's car. Sorcha was wearing a silk gown which Mum made for me years ago, along with a crown of twigs with spring flowers woven into it. Hamish wore a mesh suit of armour, a knight's helmet and carried a bejewelled sword. I was in the kitchen icing some cupcakes that Mum and I had baked the day before. The sun was shining and Dad had cut a branch of apple blossom for Sorcha to wave at our grandparents as they arrived.

"They're here!" cried Sorcha, and we all raced out to the front of Holly Cottage to form a welcoming party.

Sorcha waved the branch of blossom.

"We've got our own castle," she called as they got out of the car.

"And aren't you a lovely princess, just right for living in a castle," said Granny Berry.

Dad cleared his throat. "Em, Sarah, we don't really want the kids getting the idea that we can ever live in the castle," he said.

"Oh sure, sorry, Dan. I'm just playing along." Granny winked. "They look so cute. I remember Katie in that dress."

Mum had produced a lovely spread for afternoon tea. We had cheese and cucumber sandwiches with Victorian peach chutney, fruit scones, served with jam and whipped cream, ginger cake and iced cupcakes. The adults had a pot of tea and we had milkshakes. Before long, the chat turned to the castle.

"What are you going to do with it?" asked Grandpa Mackenzie bluntly.

"We'll have to advertise it for sale," said Dad. "We can't afford to look after it, and it's much too big for us to live in."

"And what do you think it will be bought for?" asked Granny Berry. "I mean, you guys don't want your peace and quiet to be ruined. What if it becomes a recovery clinic for nutcases or alcoholics or something?"

"Sarah," scolded Grandpa Berry. "Trust you to see the downside."

Everybody laughed, but I thought that Granny had a very good point. The castle is so close to our home and if nasty people moved in, it would be terrible. I think I realised at that point that she was firmly on my side.

"I know we often go up there at Christmas," said Grandpa Mackenzie. "But I don't really know much of the layout. Can you give us a tour of the place to refresh our rusty old memories?"

"That's a great idea," said Mum. "You might have some ideas of where we can advertise it, you know, like in hotel magazines or to spa companies or whatever? Maybe it could be a school? Who knows?"

We all trouped up to the castle, walking at Dad's pace. I found myself wondering if they would discover the ballroom — *my* ballroom. I never locked it when I left.

We walked through the big front door and stood for a few moments in the grand hall. Then we looked in all the nooks and crannies and cupboards. We took the winding stair downstairs to the servants' quarters. After we had checked out the kitchens and pantries, we came back upstairs and walked along the main corridor towards the library. Most of the rooms were unlocked but empty, yet one of the doors was still locked.

"I really must try to find a key to open that room," said Dad. "God knows what's behind that door."

I was getting tense. Would they notice that the door to the ballroom was open? The door was very much concealed by the fancy panelling, but I must have left it slightly ajar, and it caught Mum's eye as we went past.

"Hey, look. This room seems to be open," she said. "Never been in here before. Never even noticed a door here."

We all followed her into the ballroom. My heart was pounding and my mouth went dry.

"Wow! This is quite something," said Granny Mackenzie. Everyone marvelled at how beautiful it was. My eyes darted anxiously round the room. *Oh no.* I had left my *Swan Lake* tutu by the gramophone, along with my ballet shoes.

Please don't see them, I prayed.

It was Sorcha who spotted them first.

"Look!" she said, running towards the outfit. "It's a ballet room."

Mum looked at the tutu then at me. She must have recognised the tulle and swans down from her box … She looked at the gramophone. The record of *Swan Lake* was still on the turntable.

Our eyes locked. I couldn't tell if she was going to reveal my secret to everyone. Dad would go crazy if she made a fuss …

But she just gave a small smile.

"I hope you don't get cold in here," she whispered.

"Not once I'm dancing," I whispered back.

"Katie," began Sorcha, "aren't these your ..."

"Now," interrupted Mum, "let's go and see the famous secret cupboard where Katie found Dr Campbell's book of wishes. She's a sly one for secrets, y'know."

When we peered into the cupboard in the library again, I knew the box would be gone, but I was expecting to see Dr Campbell's notebooks where they had been before. But, much to my disappointment, they had vanished too.

Back in Holly Cottage, I flopped in the family room, supposedly watching *The Secret Garden* with Sorcha, while Dad and the grandpas spent ages talking about how useless the castle was to us, while Mum and the grannies were cooking in the kitchen.

"Isn't it strange how you'd think it was a fairy-tale castle, but it's actually just a crumbling old wreck," said Grandpa Berry.

"Yeah, but think what they'll make out of it when they sell it," said Grandpa Mackenzie. "I'm so pleased for you, son. Since the accident, you haven't really earned what you deserve. You were such a top chef — then fate stepped in."

They talked about how great it would be for corporate business meetings, or weddings, or spa breaks. Grandpa Berry said it would make a lovely theme park. Dad said it would make a lovely writer's retreat, where authors came to finish tricky novels. I supposed Dr Campbell would have approved of that, but I didn't want to listen to them. Dr Campbell had never wanted us to sell the castle. *Does no one understand that?* I thought.

Before supper, Granny Berry and I went to play Scrabble in a corner of the family room.

"It's a pity," she said.

"What is?"

"That we can't find a way to keep hold of the old castle. Never thought my daughter would end up owning a magical Scottish castle!"

"Yeah. I love it so much. I really want to keep it — and I know that's what Dr Campbell wanted. But what can I do?" I said.

"Y'never know, honey. You might think of something." She laughed as she cleaned up on the Scrabble board with the word: DETERMINATION.

After a yummy casserole, followed by creamy rice pudding, I went off to bed. I lay there with my fairy lights twinkling, thinking about everything. My life used to be quiet and calm; now it was a fast-flowing river rapid, and I had to keep up with it somehow.

In a way, I decided, we were no better than the young Campbells, looking forward to getting the money for the building, the bricks and mortar of the castle, instead of taking care of its spirit for Dr Campbell.

Would he have left it to us if he thought we'd sell it without a fight? I asked myself.

When I considered all the people who might come to view the castle, the way they would measure it up to see if it would suit weddings or murder-mystery weekends, I knew beyond all doubt what I wanted more than anything in the world. I had known it for many weeks. I wanted to turn it into a world-famous school of ballet, with Mum running the dance classes. That way I could get good enough for The Royal Ballet without going away from my family too soon. I knew it would be expensive to make it work, but surely somehow we could make it happen? Mum always said, *Where there's a will there's a way.* Well, we had Dr Campbell's will, so there *had* to be a way.

I just had to think it all through before I suggested it to Mum and Dad, otherwise they'd come out with loads of things I hadn't thought about. That's what they always do. I'll say something like, "Can I go to Perth on the bus on Saturday?" And they'll say, "What time's the bus? What bus are you getting back? Have you got bus fares? Do you have money to spend at the shops?

Who else is going? Is your warm coat clean? I thought you had blisters from your ballet pointes, how will you walk around the town? What would you do if you got separated from your friends?" Then after I've answered everything to their liking, they'll say, "Sure you can go, have a lovely time, and here's five pounds to get a nice little something at Claire's Accessories."

I would definitely have to be super-organised. I decided that in the morning, I'd make a scrapbook and fill it with my ideas for the ballet school. The more organised I was, the better the chance of holding on to my beloved Cloudberry Castle.

16. The Discovery

I was awake before anyone else on the Saturday morning. I opened my curtains and sat on my bed with an empty scrapbook, some gel pens, felt pens and cuttings from ballet magazines, as well as bits of ribbon, swan's down, tulle, sequins and stickers. I tried to think of all the questions which my parents would ask me when they heard about the plan for a ballet school.

Cloudberry Castle SCHOOL OF DANCE

BUSINESS PLAN BY KATIE MACKENZIE

The whole idea: The castle at Cloudberry, Lochvale, Perthshire was built in 1856 by the eighth Thane of Lochvale to replace an earlier house on the site. Since

1972, it has been owned by Dr Edmund Campbell, an expert in Egyptology, who published many books on the subject of the Pyramids of Giza. It is now owned by Mr and Mrs Dan and Beth Mackenzie of Holly Cottage, also on the cloudberry estate.

This plan shows how it could be converted perfectly into a daily and residential dance school, specialising in classical ballet, taught by Beth Mackenzie.

How will we do it? The ballroom will make an ideal dance studio, and some bedrooms, which would each sleep four girls, will be made on the upper floor. As well as this, the kitchens will need to be modernised and a comfortable sitting room will be required, with TV, table tennis and board games for evenings. Also, a few classrooms for normal schoolwork for the residential pupils will be essential.

Builders will soon estimate how much this renovation work will cost.

How long will it take? From the day we start creating the ballet school until the day it opens to pupils will take about 1 year.

6 months for building work.

3 months to get classroom teachers and other staff.

3 months to advertise the school and show round pupils.

How many dancers can we take at once? 4 residential students from the following age groups: 10-12 years, 13-15 years, 16-18 years = 12 full-time pupils. Daily dance classes for local pupils will also be held. The demand will be strong as the current ballet teacher is leaving Lochvale at the beginning of May. 20 day pupils per day.

How will we advertise? In ballet magazines, newspapers and on the internet.

How will we learn normal school subjects as well? Two teachers will give us lessons so that we can also pass school exams, in case we do not have ballet careers.

How much will it cost to stay here? It will be the same as a normal boarding school.

Costs of running it: We will have to pay the teachers, extra ballet teacher, bills for food, heating, lighting etc.

Where will the Mackenzie family live? In a flat on the first floor of the castle. This is already there and will simply need a coat of paint.

How will we pay for the renovations which will need to be made to the castle?

I scratched my head over this last question. I knew it would all cost a lot of money, long before anyone paid to be at the ballet school. And I also knew that I could not bring up the subject with Dad until I could answer this last and most important question. So far, this was nothing more than the dreams of a silly little girl.

I gazed up to the castle, looking for inspiration.

Finally an idea came into my mind: what *was* inside the one room in the castle which was still locked? If I could find the key, just maybe I would find something of great value. Maybe a vase or a painting, or a tiny little snuffbox. I saw a box worth £80,000 once at the *Antiques Road Show* when they came to Perth.

I jumped out of bed. I would go to check on Bella, and then go on a search for the keys to the locked room.

Mum was making a huge pot of porridge for everyone in the kitchen.

"Hi Katie, where are you off to this early?" she asked.

"Em, just going to check on Bella. I need to take her some fresh hay. Then I'll come straight back," I said.

"Will you, indeed?" she said, with raised eyebrows.

"Well, I might go to dance first," I admitted.

"Oh, Katie. You must eat breakfast first," she said. "And I want you to tell me everything that you get up to, darling. So that I can find you if you need help. Imagine if you had hurt yourself in the castle; we would never have thought to look in there. I will trust you if you trust me," she said.

"Deal. From now on, I'll tell you everything," I promised as I tucked into a bowl of porridge, sweetened with honey and raspberry jam. And yet, I was fibbing again already, as I didn't tell her that I was on a mission to find a valuable object to finance my ballet-school dream. My life was getting so complicated these days.

Over at the stables, Bella was pleased to see me. "I think it's time for you to go out to the meadow to graze for a little while," I told her.

She seemed to agree with that. The worst of the winter had passed. No more hats, scarves and gloves — thank goodness.

I led her out to the meadow and closed the gate behind her.

"I'll come back for you in an hour or so," I said. She began to run round the field crazily, bucking and jumping.

I was striding over to the castle when I spotted Granny Berry out walking in the grounds, taking photographs of the new leaves which were appearing on the trees. She looked up and spotted me.

"Hi, Katie, where you headed?" she asked. I made a split-second decision to tell her everything.

"Granny, can you keep a secret?" I said.

"Sure. Mum's the word," she said.

"I'm on a mission," I told her. "I think there might be something worth a lot of money in the castle. And if there is, then maybe I can persuade Mum and Dad to keep the castle."

"Come on then, what are we waiting for?" asked Granny.

"If only I could find the keys to the locked room," I said. "Who knows what might be in there."

"Let's think this through. Where do you think the old guy would keep the keys?"

"I can't think. Why don't we make our way round and you can photograph things that take our eye, and if we find the keys on our way, great?"

"Okay, sounds like a good plan," said Granny. "We can't go wrong."

We were soon inside the castle, feeling very nervous but energetic, searching cupboards, drawers and dusty, shut-up rooms. There were so many curious objects, but we had to find out if they were of any value.

"Granny, can you start taking photographs of stuff, and we can send the pictures on e-mail to antiques' experts?" I suggested.

"Sure, good idea," agreed Granny Berry. We began to snap a load of assorted items on the digital camera.

"What about this portrait?" said Granny. "It says here

it's the first Thane of Lochvale. He's kind of ugly, but someone might want it."

"Oh, definitely. Get that," I said. "That *must* be worth something."

There was soon quite a variety of items on Granny's camera: jugs, vases, miniatures, boxes, brooches and china.

"There must be one thing of value amongst this lot," said Granny, flicking though her images. "Shame we didn't find the keys though."

"Yeah, there has to be a reason he locked that room. But surely there'll be something valuable amongst this lot on your camera. Oh, but there's just one more thing I'd like to check," I remembered. "Follow me."

I ran along to the secret cupboard in the library. It was bothering me that there was no sign of Dr Campbell's notebooks when we checked it out the day before, during our tour. Maybe I was mistaken — I needed to make sure.

I raced over to the wooden panelling and opened the cupboard. It was totally empty.

"What are you searching for?" asked Granny.

"It's some notebooks. Dr Campbell used to put them in here, and they were here the night I found the box, but they've vanished."

"What was in them?" asked Granny.

"I dunno. Lots of Egyptian words. He would sit by the fire, writing and thinking."

"Hmmm. Maybe a story?" suggested Granny. "Let's look around and see what we can find."

We didn't seem to be getting anywhere. "Maybe his son took them away," I said.

I thought back to the night I had met the family in this very room. The fateful night when the box revealed Dr Campbell's surprising wishes for the castle. I pictured everyone around the room: Keira on the sofa; David over by the cupboard with me; Mum by the fireplace; and what was Mariella doing? She was ... shredding at the desk.

I went over to the big desk. There was a cardboard box full of paperwork.

"Look here, Granny," I said. "Mariella Campbell must have abandoned her shredding work, shocked by the contents of the box. There's a pile of unshredded stuff here."

Granny helped me to look through the piles of letters, cards and documents. Near the bottom, we came across a bundle of exercise books.

"These look like the notebooks, Granny," I said.

We opened one of them. "*Egyptian Scandal*. A mystery by Dr Edmund Campbell."

17. Egyptian Scandal

The notebooks seemed to contain a mystery story set in Egypt. I read a bit. It was lovely to see Dr Campbell's handwriting.

"It's about the theft of the Rosetta Stone. Sounds quite thrilling. A bit like an Indiana Jones story set in the 1930s," I said, flicking through the pages.

"Sounds pretty exciting," said Granny. "I love ancient Egypt. Especially Cleopatra, Nefertiti, Tutankhamun, all that stuff."

"Yes, it's a cool subject. Do you think the story might be valuable?" I asked.

"Might be. He's written other books, hasn't he? So he must have a good reputation in the publishing world in this area. Maybe this is the first time he's done fiction based on his research," observed Granny.

"Granny, could you help me to type up the story on the laptop, then I can print off lots of copies. Somebody might want it. And even if it isn't worth much, I'd love to do it for Dr Campbell. I think he just lost confidence in himself towards the end. I wish he had believed in it."

"Yes, it's a nice idea, but it's years since I did touch typing. I used to be fast. You could read it out to me, and I'll do my best!" said Granny.

We left the castle, with lots of beautiful images on Granny's camera and the *Egyptian Scandal* notebooks in my bag. But still no keys to the secret room.

On the way back to Holly Cottage, we went past the meadow to catch Bella. She didn't want to come indoors, but I tempted her with a handful of long grass and clipped her lead rope on to her halter.

Once Bella was safely tucked in her stable, Granny and I ambled home. I patted the exercise jotters in my bag. I couldn't believe that Mariella Campbell was planning to shred them.

"These are so precious, Granny," I said. "It's lovely to think that a part of Dr Campbell will live on forever."

"Yes, darling. Even if they are worth nothing, this is such a lovely job to do for him."

Granny and I told the others that we had to work on the Boston Tea Party project, which is exactly what we *should* have been doing. My big dreams for the castle were making me very rebellious.

After Saturday lunch, the rest of the family went off to the swimming pool in Perth, but we stayed at home to work on the "project".

Granny and I settled down at the kitchen table with the laptop and got to work.

"Right," said Granny, "I reckon we've got about four hours to get this done. Let's get cracking!"

We began to read the story aloud and it was incredibly exciting, about a quest to find the real Rosetta Stone when it was discovered that the stone in the British Museum was an elaborate fake. The clues to the whereabouts of the stone had been left in the pyramids by the adventurer who had hidden it. We just had to keep reading on to find out where it was. Every few chapters, we pieced together another clue, one at the Temple of Rameses and another at the Great Pyramid of Khufu. The story took us on a journey up the River Nile, from Cairo to Giza, on to the tombs of Beni Hasan and the ruins at Amarna. The final location was Abydos, the most sacred site in all of Egypt. We had to read the ending before we got to typing it, as it was so gripping. It had such a twist, and made me want to study everything to do with ancient Egypt.

"Granny?" I said. "Do you think if we find it exciting, other people will too?"

"Yes, Katie. That would be a fair assumption," said

Granny excitedly. "It's a cracking read."

We were just finishing reading the last few words when we heard the cars back on the drive.

"I'll start typing it later," said Granny. "But we'd better put all this away for now."

When the rest of the family walked through the door, there we were, discussing the American War of Independence, as if nothing else had been going on all day.

I was completely exhausted that night. Even after I fell asleep, and the whole house fell dark and quiet, dear Granny Berry worked away on the laptop. Throughout her stay Granny kept sneaking off to finish the typing before she went home.

Before she left for Boston, she presented me with five printed copies of the finished manuscript.

"Granny, I wish you didn't have to go home. I don't know how to thank you," I said.

"It's been a pleasure, darling. Always follow your dreams," she said. "I wish we lived here too. But Grandpa and I have to think about your cousins in Boston too, sweetie. Now, another thing: I've e-mailed a load of pictures of the treasures from the castle to some auction houses in Edinburgh. If I get any replies, I'll call you, okay?"

"Great. Surely something will bring in some money," I replied.

"Katie, I think Dr Campbell would be feeling very confident in your efforts right now," she said.

It was horrid when my grandparents left Cloudberry. I hugged them all for ages.

"Good luck with the 'Boston Tea Party'," winked Granny Berry as she got into the car.

My school project was not good, which wasn't like me at all, but I was exhausted with all the ballet-school stuff I was planning, and rehearsing for the show. I spent the bus journeys to and from school writing up stuff about the American War of Independence, and I sat in class at break and lunch too, just to get it finished. Finally, and three days late, I was able to hand in my project.

"Katie," said Mr Matthews as he took it in, "is everything okay at the moment? You're usually so prompt with your work."

"Sorry," I said.

"You don't seem yourself lately," he said.

"It's just that the ballet show is coming up," I said.

"Yes, I understand," he said. "I know you love your ballet, but don't let it use up all your energy, okay?"

"Yes, I'll try to sort myself out," I promised.

Mr Matthews looked really concerned. He's a kind man. He must have to do a lot of work at home, marking all these boring projects. I knew I was acting strangely and that he had a good point. But I still had one last job to do: I needed to send off the copies of *Egyptian Scandal* to some publishers. After that, I'd try to get back to normal.

When I got home, I asked to borrow Dad's computer and I Googled "publishers of mysteries UK". Loads of addresses came up, so I chose five at random, and wrote out their addresses neatly on big brown envelopes which I "borrowed" from Dad's desk. I included a little typed letter in with each copy of the manuscript, explaining what was enclosed. Finally, I cycled down to Mrs Renton's post office with them.

"Hi, Katie. You look busy," she said.

I passed her the envelopes.

"Anything of value in these?" she asked.

"It's a story by Dr Campbell," I admitted. She looked at the addresses.

"Tell you what, Katie dear. I'll cover the postage for you," she offered kindly. "And I'll let you know just as soon as any replies come in."

"Thank you." I smiled.

"Actually, Katie, a letter has arrived for your parents. Maybe you could give it to them?" she said.

"Yes, of course," I agreed. The postmark was Kensington, London.

The Campbells!

18. A Little Help From Your Friends

I raced home with the letter. What if it changed everything? Maybe the Campbells had found a legal way of claiming the castle back? I wished I could have ripped it open, but I could never do that. It wasn't addressed to me.

"Mum!" I called as I dashed into the kitchen. "There's a letter for you and Dad. It's from Kensington in London."

Mum was bathing Hamish. He's always filthy, but this was something else. He had been caking himself in dirt to look like a camouflaged soldier.

"I've got a letter from the post office for you," I told Mum breathlessly.

"Can I have it please, darling?" she said, drying her hands on a towel.

Her face went cloudy and distant as she looked at the envelope. She opened it very carefully and sat down by the bath. She read it through slowly. Her face did not change enough for me to guess what she was feeling.

"Well?" I said.

"I guess they've laid it to rest now," was all she said. And we've never spoken about that letter since. I can only guess that they had tried every way to reclaim the castle, but had not succeeded. I will always wonder if there were any kind words in the letter, as Mum seemed a little bit cheerier after it arrived.

By the middle of April, I was incredibly excited about the production of *Swan Lake*, which was only two weeks away. Apart from schoolwork, all I was doing was rehearsing my dances so that I would be as brilliant as possible on the big day.

We were due to have a full dress rehearsal in Perth on the coming Sunday. But I was learning that when something made me intensely happy, a sad thing often happened too. Since Dr Campbell died when I was deliriously happy in London, I was always wondering when something alarming might happen again, right out of the blue.

Even though I had hoped and prayed that Mum and Dad would change their minds about selling the castle, the FOR SALE sign went up at the end of the road on Monday the 15th of April. I desperately wanted to rip it down. But what could I do? I still couldn't answer the final, crucial question in my ballet-school business plan. How were we going to afford the renovations without a boost of cash from somewhere?

Mr Wilson, the lawyer, had made us think that there would be no buyers due to the economic recession, which cheered me a little. But the phone rang on the Tuesday afternoon when I was doing maths homework — division of fractions — at the kitchen table.

"Hello, Beth Mackenzie speaking," said Mum cheerfully.

She was nodding. "Yeah, Jamie, Saturday should be fine. Just wait until I get a pen ... twelve noon, with Mr Parker of the Liberty Hotel Group. Great news. Sounds really exciting. Thanks. Bye." She called off.

I carried on doing my homework at the table.

"Yippee. We've got a viewer already!" she said.

I was devastated. The gloom of bad luck descended on me again. *What if they love it?* I thought. It was all going out of control. There was no way I would hear back from the publishers that quickly. It had been over two weeks since I sent the manuscripts and I still hadn't heard a word. And so far, Granny Berry hadn't called with any news about the value of the treasures we'd photographed.

Maybe no one wanted an old family portrait or a slightly chipped china vase these days. But there had to be a way. All I needed was some more time.

"Who are these people who're interested in the castle, Mum?" I asked casually at breakfast on the Wednesday morning.

"It's a guy who is acting on behalf of a huge American hotel chain. They've been looking for a Scottish castle for a while."

"Sounds really promising," said Dad.

"Oh, that's great news," I said. "Are you and Dad going to show him around the castle?"

"No, we'll leave all that to Jamie, the agent," said Dad. "I'd probably say all the wrong things and put them right off."

"Yeah, probably," I agreed.

Dad ruffed up my hair for that comment. But that chat set me thinking. I went over to dance in the ballroom after school as usual, practising my steps for *Swan Lake*, but all the time I was dancing, my brain was whirring, thinking about how I could stop the viewer from wanting to buy the castle.

I began to smile as I hit on an idea. It was so obvious. I would simply *have* to make the castle as unappealing as possible.

As soon as I got back to the cottage, I called up Mallie.

"Want to help me on a mission at the weekend?" I whispered down the line.

"Yeah, sure. What's going on?" she asked.

"I'll tell you about it at school. But I'll need you over here on Saturday from about ten a.m. until after one. And do you think your muddy idiot brothers would help us out too?"

"I'll ask them. Can't wait to hear more," she replied.

Mallie and I spent the rest of the week discussing how to make the castle seem really, horribly, dreadfully awful.

Saturday morning came, and all my hard work throughout the week began to spring into action.

First off, before the Lennox gang arrived, I filled a wheelbarrow full to the brim with manure from Bella's stable.

"Hee hee, Bella. For a lovely little pony, you do make a horrible big smell. This will be locked in a cupboard and the key hidden. They'll think Cloudberry Castle has very dodgy plumbing indeed!" I told the little pony, who showed her teeth as if she was laughing too. This was so much fun.

At about ten fifteen, Mallie and her brothers, Finn and Rory, arrived at the castle from the far end of the estate. Tullyacre lies to the west of the castle. Thankfully Mum and Dad didn't see them arriving. You have to think about *everything* on a mission like this one.

127

I was delighted with the effort the boys had made. They looked like the most terrifying punks imaginable, just as I had requested. Filthy (which required no effort), with dyed red hair standing on end in a Mohican, with loads of chains and pins and huge black boots. Ideal! Even I was a bit terrified, and I knew they were just pretending.

Mallie would provide the final "down side" of the castle in the ballroom. Surely this three-phased attack would put anyone off.

"And we've got the two-way walkie-talkies. One each," said Rory. "This is an excellent mission, Katie. Respect."

Mallie had suggested the walkie-talkies as her dad and brothers always use them around the farm. A brilliant touch.

"What's first?" asked Rory.

"Well, if you guys could help me get the manure into the cupboard in the grand hall, that would be great," I said. "Only thing is, that's where you're hiding at first."

"Cheers," said Finn.

Rory and Finn pushed the wheelbarrow into place. "Thought you said it was a little pony you had," said Finn with a grimace.

"She is, but I've been saving this all week," I explained proudly.

"Eeeww. Nasty!" exclaimed Rory.

"Just get in," I told them. "I thought you two were used to farmyards."

Once Mallie was in position in the ballroom, I went up to the top of the outlook tower in the west turret with my walkie-talkie. It gave me a great view all round the castle. I would be able to see cars arriving and leaving.

"Testing, testing, can everybody hear me?" I asked over the hand-set.

"Yep, receiving, over and out," said the boys.

"And me too," added Mallie.

Jamie, the estate agent, was the first to draw up.

"First target arriving," I announced over the walkie-talkie.

19. Mission Accomplished

Jamie got out of his car. He obviously had no idea that I was watching him as he fluffed up his hair in the wing mirror of his red Mercedes. He looked very vain. He was wearing a pale pink shirt under a smart navy pinstriped suit. His shoes looked highly polished and very expensive, and his hair was over-styled. Not like my Dad, who always goes around with scruffy hair, wearing jeans or cords and knitted sweaters.

Jamie let himself into the grand hall.

"He looks a right nerd," said Rory over the walkie-talkie. He and Finn were peeking out from the keyhole in the big cupboard in the hall, ready to make their entrance in due course.

"Ssshh," I giggled. "We don't want them to hear these phone things crackling."

"Tell you what, Katie. It stinks down here," he said.

"Why, have you had an accident?" I said.

"Very funny. We'll do the jokes," said Finn.

"Shut up, everyone," I said, worried we would give ourselves away.

"Do you think a poltergeist will spook them?" whispered Mallie.

"Definitely," I assured her. "Remember to be subtle."

"Mallie? Subtle?" laughed Rory.

"SSSHHH!! Alert! The viewer, Mr Parker, is arriving!" I announced as a big car turned into the driveway. "Action stations everyone. Will give you the all-clear when both cars have exited the estate."

I was sweating with nerves. Mr Parker parked his car and got out. He was youngish, around thirty, and was dressed a bit like Jamie, but he seemed to look less ridiculous. Maybe it was because his job really did suit smart clothes like that, whereas Jamie just showed people round properties yet tried to look like he owned them. Mr Parker looked over the outside of the castle and gave a smile. *Blast!* He seemed to like the look of it.

Once he was inside the castle, I couldn't see what was going on. I was so curious. When the two men properly started the tour, I sneaked down to the gallery which surrounds the main staircase, where I could watch the drama unfold. I had a perfect view from behind a huge pillar.

"Yeah, it was built in 1856. It's a fine example of the Scottish baronial traditions, similar to the royal castle at Balmoral, on Deeside," said Jamie knowledgably.

"And what about things such as heating and plumbing?" said the American man.

"Well, obviously it's a little old-fashioned at the moment," said Jamie.

"Old-fashioned?" said Mr Parker in a heavy American accent. "Smells like a darned herd of cows lives in here."

Jamie coughed nervously. "Moving along, please do notice the ornate plasterwork ceilings," he said, sounding very flustered. "It's the work of the famous Finlay Carruthers."

Just then, Rory and Finn appeared, as if from nowhere, with empty cans of lager in their hands.

"Oi, this is our place," shouted Rory. "What you doin' here? Did anyone invite you?" Finn looked on menacingly.

This was brilliant! They were made for this role.

"I'm sorry about this," Jamie apologised to Mr Parker. "These local youths must have dropped in as it's unoccupied, but I can assure you, there isn't a genuine problem with squatters here."

"I'm trying to believe you, Jamie," said Mr Parker. "But this place is not what I expected from the brochure.

You guys sure know how to dress things up. It stinks, and it obviously has intruders. I'm not liking this place, Jamie, I gotta tell you."

I was so pleased I almost punched the air, but I didn't want to risk getting noticed.

"Please bear with me; there are so many lovely features to see. The exquisite ballroom, for example. You must see that," said Jamie.

I knew Mallie was in there, ready to billow the curtains around and pull a few ornaments to the floor creepily on the invisible threads we had tied to them.

I didn't see it happen, but she must have done a great job, because after a few moments in the ballroom, Jamie and Mr Parker ran out of the castle and into their cars at breakneck speed. I dashed back up to the lookout tower in time to see the two cars whiz out of the estate.

"Nice work everyone. They've gone," I said over the walkie-talkie. "Coming down to meet you all in the grand hall."

When I got down there, we all fell about laughing and high-fived each other.

"Katie, you're a lucky girl, owning a castle like this," said Finn. "No wonder you want to keep it."

"I know. Let's hope we will own it for a while to come," I said. "And thanks to you, we just might. Mr Parker was not impressed."

"We'd better get back to Tullyacre," said Mallie. "We've got lambs to feed. And Dad doesn't even know we're away."

"Well, don't scare the lambs with those hairstyles," I said to the boys.

"See you tomorrow for the ballet rehearsal in Perth," said Mallie.

"Yeah. Bus leaves at two o'clock, doesn't it? See you down in the village," I replied as I waved them off.

I took the stinking wheelbarrow back to the stables. It was going to take a few days for that smell to die down in the grand hall.

When everything was done, and Bella was fed and watered, I let myself quietly back into Holly Cottage. Mum and Dad were chatting in the kitchen.

"I thought Jamie would have waited and given us some feedback," said Dad.

"I know. That was really weird, the way they both went shooting out of the estate," agreed Mum.

"Yeah. He'll probably give us a call on Monday. Maybe he's got another property to show now. It's not as if the castle is the only property on his books," said Dad.

I felt so guilty, but nicely confident that we had done an excellent job of scaring them off. All Mum and Dad needed was some confidence that we could afford to take on the castle, and I was very much hoping to provide that. I needed one piece of good luck to bring the plan together.

20. Mixed Fortunes

I was so excited about the dress rehearsal for *Swan Lake*. We were going over to Perth Theatre to work out how we would make all our entrances and exits, and what size the stage was, and where the spotlights would shine brightest.

The bus was waiting in the village square on Sunday when Mum took me into Lochvale. There were loads of girls with lovely buns and pink ballet cardigans, waiting to get on.

"My goodness," said Mum. "Ballet really is popular in this village. What on earth will we do when Mrs Miller goes off to Australia?"

"Yeah. I can't imagine my life without ballet," I said as I kissed her goodbye.

Mallie and I sat next to each other on the bus.

"Hey, that was fun yesterday, wasn't it?" she said. "I reckon we've got rid of Mr Parker, don't you?"

"Yeah, definitely. I wonder what Jamie will say to Mum and Dad about it though."

"Just pretend you know nothing about it," said Mallie. "Nobody saw you."

I nodded, but I felt horribly guilty.

When we got to the theatre, Mrs Miller was busy setting up rails of fluffy costumes, while some of her friends were painting gorgeous scenery. The backdrop for the opening scene of the birthday party was a magnificent fairy-tale castle. It looked a bit familiar.

Mrs Miller caught me looking at it. "Ah, Katie! We used a photograph of Cloudberry Castle for this. What do you think of it?"

"It's lovely, Mrs Miller," I replied. And it was. It seemed to sparkle and shimmer, and the four fairy-tale turrets, along with the clock tower, were just right.

I was in my element that afternoon. The whole team of people helping to produce the ballet were so dedicated, and it was lovely to be a part of it. We were taken round to the dressing rooms, where there were a few seamstresses wandering about with measuring tapes round their necks and pin cushions in their hands. Our names were called out from a list, and we were all fitted for our costumes and headwear.

"Wait until you see the Swan Princess outfit," said one lady when it was my turn and she found out I was dancing Odette. It was covered over by plastic to protect it, and she slowly peeled the cover off. I was speechless. The top section of the dress was made from winter-white duchesse satin, with silky ribbon straps over the shoulders. The neckline was decorated with softest swan's down, while the skirt was longer than most tutus, with many layers of tissue-like ivory tulle.

"It's perfect," I gasped. "Can I try it on?"

"Of course you can," said the seamstress. "We want to see how it fits."

I hardly recognised myself in the mirror once it was on. I was just like Anya Swarovsky at Covent Garden. And then came the headdress — a cross between a delicate diamond tiara and a feather crown. All the girls came to see me in the outfit.

"Wow!" said Mallie. "You look like a professional." Even the meaner girls agreed it was a fabulous costume. Sadly, I had to take it all off again, and it was whisked away for tucks and tweaks. But all the tiny details of it were imprinted on my mind.

The dance practice went well, even though Mrs Miller was a bit tetchy, shouting more than normal. We found it hard getting used to all the space we had.

"Bigger steps, girls!" she cried. "*Grands jetés!* We've got lots of space."

Ballet makes me feel so alive. And when I dance, I forget about everything else.

But on the bus ride back to Lochvale, reality hit me again, and I felt guilty about being so dishonest with Mum and Dad. If they found out what I'd done over at the castle the day before, they would be so disappointed in me.

I was edgy at school all day on the Monday. At the end of the day, I dived off the school bus and rushed into the cottage to see what had happened about Mr Parker, the American viewer.

Only Dad was there. Apparently Mum and the two little ones were out flying a kite by Lily's Lake.

"Any news from Jamie about the viewer at the castle?" I asked Dad, as innocently as I could.

"Yes, actually," laughed Dad. "The guy who viewed it definitely wants to buy it, as he thinks it's got character. Wait for this, Katie. He thinks it's haunted — by a poltergeist. Isn't that just hilarious?" laughed Dad. "He seems to think he can make a 'unique selling point' out of the fact it has a ghost. Looks like an offer might be coming through in the next two weeks or so."

Dad started to whistle as he chopped plum tomatoes

139

and basil for one of his delicious homemade Margherita pizzas.

My heart sank. All that effort at the weekend, and I had ended up *encouraging* the buyer, not putting him off. I couldn't believe it; I was so disappointed. And annoyed with myself. *You're an idiot, Katie Mackenzie*, I told myself. At least my guilt faded a bit. I had accidentally helped Mum and Dad to sell the castle. Only I could manage that.

That evening, Mum was worried about me, as I was moping around moodily, which wasn't like the old me at all.

"Katie, you seem very down in the dumps, darling," she said. "I thought you'd be delighted about the ballet show. Your outfit sounds heavenly. But I saw Mr Matthews at lunchtime when I collected Sorcha, and he said you've not been yourself for weeks. What's wrong?"

I wanted to tell her about my dreams for the castle, and all that I had done to keep it in our hands, but I thought I'd better not. The childish dream of saving the castle was slipping away from me, and I was starting to come to terms with that.

"I'm just sad about Mrs Miller moving away, that's all," I said.

Mum nodded. "Yes, I must admit, it is a worry. We do need to have ballet lessons in Lochvale. The number of girls in the show just proves how popular it is round here, and there isn't that much else to do hobby-wise. I had hoped Sorcha would enjoy as many years of ballet as you have."

I nodded sadly.

I went to bed early and read my book about the history of Sadler's Wells Theatre. I had meddled in adult things I didn't understand, and I was convinced that my good luck had run out. I had given up looking out for a letter from one of the publishers. Perhaps I had been silly to think they would write back. It was time for me to go back to my old ways, of reading about girls with exciting lives rather than trying to be one.

21. No More Secrets

The very next day Mrs Renton was waiting for me when I got off the school bus. I saw that she was carrying an envelope and my heart suddenly fluttered with excitement.

"A letter for you, Katie! With a London post mark," she whispered.

I stood at the gates to Cloudberry Castle and read the letter again and again. It was from a lady called Mary Bernard at a publishers in London, Nicholson Books.

Mary Bernard • Senior Commissioning Editor
Nicholson Books • 46 Gordon Square • London • SW1 2PC
Tel: 0207 278 432

18 April

Dear Miss Mackenzie,

EGYPTIAN SCANDAL
Thanks for sending us the exciting manuscript by the late,

great Dr Edmund Campbell. I was instantly inspired by the text, and I have spent the last few weeks working on the possibility of a publishing programme for the book both in the UK and overseas.

I am delighted to be able to give you some good news. We have a great deal of enthusiasm for the work, and we are now close to making an offer for the worldwide rights to it.

You do not say if you are a literary agent or a family member. I wonder if you could call me on the number above in order to discuss the best way to move forward to publication.

Yours sincerely,

Mary Bernard

I was so excited, I hugged Mrs Renton and started dancing all the way down the road to Holly Cottage.

"Don't dance into a tree, Katie," she called. I pirouetted my way up our front path and danced up to my bedroom. I put the letter under my pillow for safe keeping, but knew that I had to involve Mum now. This letter changed everything. It provided an answer to the last part of the business plan, where a gap had been left. This could be how we would pay for the renovations. I was dying to tell Granny Berry the news, but first, I had to tell Mum.

I waited for the right moment to arise. By a stroke of luck, Dad took the two little ones out to feed the ducks on the lake before tea, while I helped Mum in the kitchen.

"Mum, I've been thinking about something," I began.

"Thought so. What's on your mind, honey?"

"Well ..." I took a deep breath, and it all came tumbling out. About the ballet-school dream, the business plan, Dr Campbell's manuscript, Granny typing it and taking photographs of the treasure, and the letter from Mary Bernard at Nicholson Books.

Mum sat down by the stove, staring at the flames. She was quiet for ages.

"I thought we said no more secrets? And as for Granny Berry, I'll be having words with her. I thought she was typing up a project about the Boston Tea Party."

"Don't be angry with Granny. She didn't offer, I asked her," I said.

"Okay, I'll call this publishing lady," she said finally, with a glint in her eye. "But it will have to be an awfully big offer to make Dad change his mind, darling," she warned.

I was ecstatic. It was so nice to be open with Mum. And there seemed to be a spark of excitement about her. I ran to fetch Mary Bernard's letter from under my pillow. My luck had changed again.

Mum called Mary Bernard while I was at school the next day. She was full of news about the call when I got home.

"Come out to the garden and help me bring the washing in, Katie." She winked.

I was dying to hear what was said.

"Well?" I asked.

"Mary Bernard thinks this book could be the bestseller of the decade. She is wildly enthusiastic about it," began Mum.

"Told you Granny and I thought it was brilliant," I said.

"Anyway, she says that she will make an offer within the next three to four weeks and that we will not be disappointed. That must mean it'll be a big offer."

"Yippee!" I cried and threw my arms around Mum.

"The only thing is, Katie, that Mr Parker is getting close to making an offer for the castle. Let's hope we hear from Mary Bernard before Dad accepts an offer."

My face fell. "What if the castle is sold just before we hear about a massive offer for the book?" I asked.

"It could happen, darling, but I will try to come up with little obstacles for the lawyers, although that can't go on forever," she explained.

"How much do you think Mary will pay?" I wondered.

"Katie, I simply don't know. It could be three thousand pounds or three million! But, you know, even if we pull this off, what are we going to do then? We don't even have a plan of action for your ballet-school idea."

"Actually, Mum. We do," I revealed. "Come up to my room and I'll show you."

I went ahead of her and pulled out my scrapbook from under the bed.

Mum was waiting in the doorway.

"Here, read this," I said.

She took the book and sat by my dressing table. She looked amazed as she turned over one page after another.

"Can I take this away to study it all?" she asked.

"Yes. I hope it makes sense. I don't want anyone to find mistakes in it," I replied. "Especially Dad."

"I'll check it over, honey. You want this really badly, don't you?" she said.

I nodded. "And I won't suddenly go off the idea, Mum. I'm devoted to ballet. And when Mrs Miller has gone, I'll be so sad. The last thing I want to do is go away to ballet school in London."

"I don't want that yet either. It would break my heart. Let me study this and see what we've got here," she said.

"Thanks, Mum. And I'm sorry for keeping secrets," I said.

"Oh, Katie. Maybe I should have opened my eyes a bit wider to the possibilities with the castle. Don't blame yourself, sweetie."

Mum came to collect me after school the next day.

"Mum! What a surprise. You never pick me up," I said, thinking how lovely Mum looked. She was wearing a deep purple dress which was covered with little sprigs of flowers, and an emerald green coat, tied at the waist with velvet ribbon. The black patent boots which I love finished off her outfit well, along with her big mauve handbag.

"I know. And I feel bad about it. But Dad is with the other two, so I thought we could go to Rosie's teashop for a chat today."

"Brilliant. I'd love that. Their cakes are delicious."

We linked arms and wandered through the village.

Inside the teashop, we were shown to a table by the window. We sat down, ordered our snacks and Mum started to chat.

"You know what?" she began. "Reading your plan has made me feel so alive and energetic today. Maybe I've got into a Mummy rut a bit over the last few years. All I do is childcare, housework and cooking. But the thought of going back to my ballet? That's really exciting, and if I could help you and Sorcha to enjoy it for longer, and contribute to the local community too, what with Mrs Miller going, then maybe, just maybe this whole plan of yours is actually a stroke of genius."

I was thrilled, stunned into silence.

She carried on. "As you say in the plan, we could have weekly lessons and a residential school as well. That way our senior residential girls could help to teach a lot of the junior classes, which would take the financial pressure off a bit. That's how ballet schools tend to work."

"Oh, Mum. I'm so pleased you love the idea," I said finally.

"Of course, you know we still have one big problem," said Mum.

"Dad?" I said.

"Exactly. I haven't mentioned it yet. He's so worried about the upkeep of the castle, and with his disability he gets so frustrated when he can't get involved with physical work in the way he used to do. I can remember a time when he would have been the first person to tackle the nitty-gritty — ordering a skip, handling the renovations, painting the walls on tall ladders." She became a little tearful, but brightened up quickly.

"What exactly happened, Mum? You know, with the accident? No one has ever really explained it to me and I can't remember much about it," I said.

"We try not to dwell on it. It was about this time of year. He went off to work at his little restaurant, *Dan's*, on Queen Street in Edinburgh. It was just five minutes away from our flat on Abercromby Place. He kissed you and me goodbye with a spring in his step. It was Saturday morning. He was going to do the lunch shift and prep things for evening, but come home for your bathtime, which is what he loved to do. Then he'd go back much later in the evening to check everything was going well. I got a telephone call about an hour after he'd left us.

Apparently, a car had hit him on Hanover Street, and he was taken to the Royal Infirmary." Mum gulped at this point. I had never seen her talk like this. She and Dad never made too much fuss about the accident.

"Did you go to visit him straight away?" I asked.

"Well, more or less. But I had to call Granny and Grandpa Mackenzie first. They were in a dreadful state. Their neighbour, Veronica, very kindly offered to come and look after you. You were only eighteen months old. So I jumped in a cab as soon as Veronica came to keep an eye on you."

"And how was he — when you first saw him?"

"Terrible. Just a mess. He was unrecognisable. But day by day, he recovered. He was young, strong and very determined. Before long, he was walking with a stick. It was a miracle, really. I suppose the lasting sadness is that he never did make that last little bit of recovery, back to his old self. But we are so grateful that he survived. It made life so precious to us. That's why we moved up here. We didn't want too much pressure on him to maintain the city lifestyle. We sold the restaurant, and we saw this cottage advertised down in Mrs Renton's post office when we were driving through Lochvale on a little tour of Perthshire."

"Gosh, I didn't know any of that," I said. "I did wonder how we ended up here. I used to think we'd been sent here to take care of Dr Campbell."

"Maybe we had," said Mum. "Anyway, you should know these things now, darling. You're so mature. You've grown up so much this year. Or at least, I've noticed it for the first time."

"I feel quite grown-up now really. And as Dad said to me at Christmas, I've realised things do change," I said.

"Yeah," said Mum, with a sigh. "But can we change Dad's point of view about this castle sale? It's up to me to win him round. But it won't be easy, Katie. And I can't guarantee the outcome, darling. Your father is a proud and stubborn man. I'll have to choose my moment carefully. I'll try to wait until I have some figures through from Mary Bernard at Nicholson Books."

22. The Performance

Over the next week or so, I kept quiet and prepared for the ballet show, hoping and praying that Mr Parker's offer for the castle would be slower than Mary Bernard's offer for Dr Campbell's manuscript.

The weekend of the show was fast approaching and on the Thursday before it, Dad went over to Loch Fyne to review two hotels and three restaurants for a summer holiday guide in the *Scotsman* newspaper.

"Don't be late for the show on Sunday," I warned him as he left on Thursday at teatime.

"I promise I'll be there. I wouldn't miss my girls for anything," he said. "I'm going to have an early lunch at the Loch Fyne Hotel, then I'll be straight over to Perth for half three, sharp. Have I ever let you down?"

"No, but I do know that you'd rather watch paint dry

than watch ballet, so I can't be sure," I said.

He tooted as he left Holly Cottage behind. Halfway up the road, he rolled down the window and called back to us, "Did you say there was something happening on Sunday?" He smiled.

Sorcha, Hamish and I ran after the car to tell him off for teasing, but we couldn't catch it.

My last chance to practise in the ballroom was after school on Friday.

"Would you come and watch me, Mum?" I asked as I got ready to go over.

"I'd love to, Katie," she said. "I'll call Mrs Renton and see if she could pop down to look after Hamish. Sorcha could come over with us. She'd like that."

Half an hour later, we were in the ballroom. Mum, Sorcha and me, all wearing ballet shoes and all dancing to Tchaikovsky.

"Lovely work, girls," said Mum. "I'm so proud of you both."

"I wish we could dance in here all the time," exclaimed Sorcha. Mum and I exchanged a smile.

"Do I look anything like Anya Swarovsky?" I asked as I pirouetted round the room.

"No, you look more like Angelina Ballerina," giggled Sorcha.

"Thanks very much," I said sarcastically. "I'll have to get you back for that."

I lifted her up and threw her over my shoulder, calling out, "Who'd like a sack of potatoes?"

She squealed happily — cheeky little monkey.

The show preparations had allowed me to forget the plans for the castle for a while, but I was still looking forward to hearing more from Mary at Nicholson Books. When I came down for breakfast on the Saturday morning, just a day before we headed up to Perth for the performance, I saw a letter lying on the hall carpet. When I examined it, I saw that it was the same sort of letter as the one Mrs Renton had brought to me. I gave it to Mum. She opened it and read it carefully. I was dying to know the news!

"She says she has cash coming in from Australia and America, and can make a very exciting offer!" said Mum

"Shall we call Dad and tell him?" I asked.

"Not yet. Wait until I see him in person," said Mum. "Just concentrate on the performance for now, Katie."

Sunday arrived, the day I had waited for. Granny and Grandpa Mackenzie pulled up at Holly Cottage in time for a late breakfast. I was sad that Granny Berry would miss the ballet, but they couldn't afford to come back again so soon.

"You must eat something, Katie," ordered Mum. "Many ballerinas collapse through hunger. Have some scrambled eggs on toast and some fresh fruit too."

Hamish was really bugging me by standing on a chair and dangling his Action Men on bungee ropes over the table. Thanks goodness Mrs Renton arrived to collect him, otherwise I might have dangled him from a bungee rope over the banister.

"Come on, Sorcha," I said, after eating as much as my nervous tummy would allow. "Time to put your hair up!" I couldn't wait to see her in her cygnet outfit. It was similar to my dress, but dinkier and much cuter. Luckily her hair do went perfectly first time, as it was soon time to go.

"Come on, girls!" called Mum. "Mrs Miller wants you at the theatre by twelve thirty. We'd better get going."

My tummy was doing flips all the way to Perth. *What if I mess up? Maybe I'll forget a dance step. Maybe I'll fall when I go up on my pointes.* All these thoughts were going through my mind.

Finally we arrived and while Mum was parking, Sorcha and I ran into the dressing rooms. Everyone was having so much fun that I began to relax. It looked like the scene I saw on the news from London Fashion Week. We were having our faces made up, (yippee — make-up!), our hair done and our costumes fitted. Everywhere you looked there was lipstick, tulle, tiaras, lights and satin shoes. Girls were giggling and Mrs Miller's cheeks were flushed pink with nerves and pride.

Time seemed to fly and soon the bell rang to tell us that the show was about to begin. I took my place on centre stage and tried to regulate my breathing. I desperately wanted Dad to be proud of me. But as the lights dimmed in the auditorium and the curtains swished back to reveal the scene on stage, I couldn't see him in the audience. My heart sank. It meant so much to me that Dad saw me dance. It was actually so dark that I couldn't see anyone I knew.

I threw myself into the first act, unsure of whether or not he was there, which made me feel tense and distracted.

23. Dancing to My Tune

At some point during the Dance of the Cygnets, the lighting changed and the audience lit up. I saw that Dad *was* sitting in the audience — near the front. Now, I was free to relax and lose myself in the ballet. I danced as though my life depended on it, and all those hours in the ballroom of Cloudberry Castle paid off. I was hardly off stage, but when I was having my make-up touched up at the interval, Mrs Miller came to see me.

"I've been passed a note for you, Katie," she said, handing me a folded scrap of paper.

It was Dad's writing. I unfolded it.

Got here with a minute to spare. Think you are awesome.
So proud of you, darling! Love you with all my heart. Dad.

I felt a warm glow inside. I put the note in my ballet case. That would definitely go in the memory box. It was time to go back out for the second half — the part of the story which carries so much emotion.

Dad's words inspired me, and I danced as if I was Anya Swarovsky. Every jump and spin went perfectly, my timing was immaculate and my passion for dance carried me along. The audience saw the tale unravel, from the curse which made Odette spend daytimes as a swan, through to her untimely end. By the time I lay on the stage as the tragic Swan Princess, I felt exhausted but elated.

The music stopped, and the applause began. It was thunderous. I stood up and curtsied, along with the rest of the dancers. We were thrilled with our performance. We were given a standing ovation, and the clapping went completely through the roof when I presented Mrs Miller with a bouquet of white lilies. All of the girls sobbed a little when she made a farewell speech.

"I am so proud of my girls," she said. "They are the finest dancers and the loveliest children. I will miss them all."

I knew that Mum would be proud of me, and Granny and Grandpa Mackenzie too, but most of all, I wanted to see Dad's face. I scanned the faces in his row and saw him. He was standing, clapping, and it looked as if tears of pride were rolling down his cheeks.

When Mrs Miller dismissed us after the show, we all went to the foyer, where a little party was underway. I ran into Dad's arms.

"Did you like it?" I asked him.

"Like it? I LOVED it, sweetheart," he said. "I wasn't bored for one second. It was magical. You took me to another place. I am so very proud of you."

I was delighted that he felt this way. I could tell he wasn't faking it, like he sometimes does. All of my effort had been worth it.

Mrs Miller approached us.

"She's very gifted, you know," she said. "She could get into any ballet school in the country. You really should think about it, Dan."

Dad nodded. "She's a star in the making, I can see that. Just like her mother."

Dad drove me back to Cloudberry, while Mum drove Sorcha. Granny and Grandpa said they had loved the show too, but they had to drive straight back to Edinburgh.

Later on, once Hamish and Sorcha were in bed, Mum and Dad discussed my performance. I watched TV, with my aching feet in a bucket of iced water.

"We can't send her away to ballet school at her age," said Dad.

"No, I couldn't bear that," said Mum. "She belongs here with us. We moved up here to spend our life with our children, didn't we?"

I could tell that Mum was itching to tell Dad about the publishing news from Mary Bernard. I crossed my fingers while she raised the subject.

"Oh, there was bit of news came through yesterday, Dan," she said casually. "Katie found an unpublished story of Dr Campbell's, called *Egyptian Scandal*, and sent it off to five publishers. We've had the first offer through. For three hundred thousand pounds."

Dad went quiet. "That changes things a bit," he said softly.

"Yes," said Mum. "Katie had the idea that Cloudberry could become a ballet school. She's made a plan. It's quite wonderful, Dan. It has really inspired me. Would you look at it?"

I held my breath while I waited for his response.

"After Katie's performance today, I've got to. I've been a fool. She has a gift, and I've never taken time to help her, Beth. Some father I've been."

"Dan, you're a wonderful father," said Mum.

I turned up the TV and stopped eavesdropping at that point. From that moment I knew that Dad was on board. Yes!

It was now the Easter holidays, thank goodness. I slept all morning on the Monday after the show. Every part of me was sore and tired, even my eyeballs. I didn't even think about rehearsing in the ballroom. Maybe I had been practising so hard to impress Dad. I'm not sure. But he *had* been impressed, and I knew it had all been worth it.

On the Monday afternoon, he drove down to meet Mr Wilson and Jamie at the lawyer's office in Lochvale. I sat at the kitchen table eating a huge bowl of leek and potato soup with crunchy croutons. It was my fourth meal of the day. I was ravenous.

"What's he going to do down there?" I asked.

"He's going to try and halt the sale of the castle to Mr Parker's Liberty Hotel Group," she said. "He's seen your plan and he loves the idea."

I gulped. It seemed like make-believe.

But as soon as we saw Dad's face on his return, we knew the news wasn't good.

"Well?" said Mum as he walked into the kitchen.

"I'm sorry, Beth. The missives have been concluded, which means there's no way back now. The castle has been sold to the Liberty Group for £250,000."

I almost fainted. It couldn't be the end of the line. I refused to believe it. Surely there was something that could be done?

"Are you quite sure, Dan?" asked Mum.

"If there was anything I could do, I would. I promise you," he replied.

Dad glanced over at me and gave a sympathetic smile. I was distraught.

I went to my room to think everything through. Now that we were all agreed on the ballet-school idea, it seemed so cruel that the chance was taken from us.

When I went out to feed Bella, I headed over to the castle. Maybe Dr Campbell would give me a sign of what to do.

But when I got there, it was different. It felt cold and empty of feelings. I thought that going in the ballroom might help. Nothing. No voices and no ideas came to me. I walked along to the library and sat on Dr Campbell's chair. Silence. Dr Campbell wasn't talking to me because we had failed to keep hold of Cloudberry. We had let him down. We had cashed in, just like his own family had wanted to do. But Dr Campbell had thought the Mackenzies were better than that.

24. The Swans

I didn't dance at all over the next few days. Mallie and I rowed on Lily's Lake, we listened to music, and we took a bus into Perth … anything to take my mind off the loss of the castle and the end of my dreams.

While Mallie and I were waiting at the bus stop in Lochvale, we saw a huge removal van at Mrs Miller's cottage on the square. Our beloved ballet teacher was leaving us forever. Everything was coming to an end.

Of course, it was lovely that we had got a deal for *Egyptian Scandal,* but the money alone meant nothing without the dance-school dream. Mum and Dad were quiet and thoughtful. I didn't want to blame Dad for the outcome. He was suffering enough. Sure, it would be nice to have £250,000, but I think he realised that the dance school would have bonded us all together and given us the same goal.

I found Dad in the family room one day, looking through my little business plan for Cloudberry.

"I'm proud of you, love, for creating this," he said. "But it would have been an awful lot of work, you know. Mum could still start a little dance school down in the village hall. We'll be able to afford the rent no problem once the castle is sold. I think she's got her heart set on running a ballet school. She's ready for the challenge. I'll work less and do more with Hamish and Sorcha so Mum can have more of a life."

"Dad, don't you see that it's about respecting Dr Campbell's wishes, not just having a ballet school *anywhere*," I explained.

"Katie, I understand exactly what you mean. Only, it's too late," he said. "I should have seen it sooner." I thought I saw his eyes looking misty. Dad hardly ever cries. I couldn't bear it.

During the Easter holidays, Mum half-heartedly began to consider taking over from Mrs Miller in the village hall. Meanwhile, Granny e-mailed to say that Bonhams auction rooms in Edinburgh were finally coming over to value the treasures she had sent by photograph.

Mary Bernard from Nicholson Books called Mum to say that the book required very little editing and that it was due for publication just before Christmas, simultaneously in London and New York. There was even talk of a film already. All these pieces of news should have filled us with joy, yet our hearts were heavy. Even Hamish and Sorcha were quite subdued.

By the end of the Easter holiday, spring had fully arrived at Cloudberry. Bella was out in the meadow the whole time, and the trees were lush green again. It should have been a time of such joy, but life at Holly Cottage was very sad.

I cycled round the estate on the Sunday before we went back to school, with Sorcha in the trailer.

"What's wrong with everybody, Katie?" she asked. "It's been rubbish here since we started to own the castle."

Poor little Sorcha. It must have been so confusing for her. I was confused, and I understood, or had even caused, most of what had gone on lately.

"Sorcha, owning the castle is okay, it's the way that we've dealt with owning the castle that's the problem," I said. "We haven't respected Dr Campbell's wishes." And as I said that, a flock of white swans flew above our heads and landed on Lily's Lake.

"Look at that, Sorcha!" I exclaimed.

"Swans! I've never seen swans here before."

"Same here," I replied, deep in thought. Swans on the lake. Maybe it was a sign.

It was the middle of the next week when we got the news through. I only heard it by accident at first — as usual. Mum and Dad should never become secret agents as they are always discussing private things at full volume. They thought I was down at the meadow, but I was actually reading the problem page in my magazine in the family room.

"Don't get her hopes up until we're quite sure," said Mum.

"Oh, Beth, I hope I can give her faith in me again with this. It's a miracle," said Dad.

"Who'd have thought Dr Campbell would have thought of everything."

"Katie would," said Dad. "She trusts him with all her heart."

I knew then that somehow everything would be okay. Dr Campbell had sent the swans to show me that I could dance as the swan forever at Cloudberry Castle.

It was two days later when I found out exactly what had happened. As soon as I knew, I called Mallie to fill her in.

"Hey, Mal, guess what? Dr Campbell had written in the title deeds that the castle cannot be used as a business unless it will directly benefit the residents of Lochvale. The lawyers ruled that a fancy hotel would not be for the use of local people, therefore, planning permission was denied at the council! The Liberty Hotel Group has pulled out of the deal at the last minute. We still own the castle."

"Yippeee!" she shrieked. "I so want a friend with a castle."

"I'm so happy. I feel like I've got a guardian angel," I told her.

"I think you do," said Mallie. "But, there's just one thing."

"What's that?"

"No more dramas for a while, okay? I'm exhausted," she said.

"*You're* exhausted?" I replied with a giggle.

Dad took over the whole Cloudberry Castle project, and it seemed to fire him up with all this energy, which I've never seen in him before. Maybe I imagined it, but it was as though he was walking a little bit faster, and holding his back a little bit straighter. I had to get back into my schoolwork, but I knew that everything was in good hands. The advance cheque arrived from Nicholson Books, and the valuer came over from Bonhams auction rooms in Edinburgh one sunny Saturday afternoon in the middle of May.

Dad and I went over to meet him. He was a very posh man called Miles Corton-Fox. He was dressed in marmalade coloured cords, with a tweed jacket, striped shirt, busy tie and loud spotty handkerchief.

"Crikey. Did he get dressed in the dark?" Dad whispered to me as we let him into the castle.

"Sshhh," I giggled. "That's cheeky."

Miles buzzed around making notes in a book.

"Some rather nice paintings," he mumbled. "One or two interesting trinkets. Might make a thousand or two."

"I wish we could see in this locked room," said Dad. "But we can't find the keys anywhere."

"Why not call round a locksmith to take off the lock?" suggested Miles.

"Nice thinking, Miles," said Dad, getting out his mobile phone.

Within the hour, a local handyman, Archie Stuart, was on the scene. He managed to remove the lock, and when the door was pushed open, we all stood open-mouthed.

Behold ... the Egyptology room!

The room looked just like how I imagined the inside of one of the pyramids to be. Papyrus lay on a gold chest, folded and tied with ribbons. There were wooden statues, engraved gold bracelets, a carved golden hawk and archaeologist's tools.

"Look at this. Isn't it the Rosetta Stone?" I exclaimed.

"No," said Miles. "But unless I'm very much mistaken, it's part of another stone, the Luxor Stone. This part has been missing for many years," said Miles. "All these things are of great historical importance. A museum would love to show these as exhibits. How jolly exciting." Miles managed to sell the artefacts to the National Museum of Scotland for an awful lot of money. Mum made out a very big cheque to David Campbell and posted it to an address in Kensington. She felt properly happy after that.

With each passing day, as spring turned to summer and the air at Cloudberry became scented with rose petals, more architects, workmen and designers arrived over at the castle. I was busy with schoolwork, but when the summer holidays began, I was able to help out every day.

The bedrooms in the castle were painted a pretty colour called Ballet Shoe Pink. A wonderful new kitchen was installed, just like the sort in hotels. It's all stainless steel, with huge cookers and sinks. Oh, and the TV room was created — very cool, with colourful sofas and a wide screen TV!

The castle was transformed and brightened up so much that it was hardly recognisable. And the best moment of all was when a massive mirror and barre was fitted in the ballroom. I knew at that moment that it wasn't a dream; it was really happening. Now I had all the space I needed to perfect my dancing.

The Cloudberry Castle School of Dance was due to be open for business in ten months. It was time to advertise for full-time students, tutors and local dancers. And I knew the bittersweet day would come when we would move into the castle and leave Holly Cottage behind.

One day towards the end of summer, Sorcha and I stood in the ballroom of the castle, dressed in our *Swan Lake* outfits. We looked out to Lily's Lake. The swans looked up at us, seemed to nod and glided gracefully over the lake. Everything was going to work out fine. Dr Campbell was still looking after us.

Janey Louise Jones
Author Interview

Q: Cloudberry Castle is all about a little girl who loves ballet? Why did you decide to write a book about ballet?

Janey Louise Jones [JJ]: Ballet was my favourite hobby in childhood and I still find watching a performance of ballet absolutely magical.

Q: What inspired you to become an author?

JJ: I have written stories for as long as I can remember and it was natural for me to write as a career.

Q: What was your favourite book and who was your favourite author when you were a child?

JJ: When I was a child I loved The Secret Garden by Frances Hodgson Burnett.

Q: Cloudberries are special in this book but not a lot of people have heard of them. What are cloudberries?

JJ: Cloudberries are a bit like golden coloured raspberries and they are full of vitamin C. They have a sharp taste, which is delicious in jams and juices.

Q: In Cloudberry Castle, Katie's favourite ballet is Swan Lake. Do you have a favourite ballet?

JJ: I love Swan Lake too as it is so beautiful on stage, and very emotional. But I also love The Nutcracker, by the same composer, Tchaikovsky.

Q: The Cloudberry estate is near Perth in Scotland. Why did you decide to set your book there?

JJ: I think that Perthshire is the most beautiful part of the United Kingdom, where real life meets fairy tales.

Q: As well as writing Cloudberry Castle you have written lots of Princess Poppy books. Do you have a favourite book?

JJ: No, I am equally proud of all my stories and would never do a book that I don't love.

Q: Who is your favourite character from Cloudberry Castle?

JJ: Katie, the heroine, is my favourite character. She is brave and never gives up on her dreams.

Q: Are the characters in Cloudberry Castle based on anyone you know?

JJ: I named Katie in the book after my niece, also called Katie Mackenzie. However, all the characters are made up, and I tend to avoid using personalities based on friends and family in case anyone feels it's too personal.

Q: If you hadn't been an author what do you think you would have been instead?

JJ: I was a teacher for a while and I enjoyed that too. But I would have loved to be a ballerina.

Q: What is the best part of being an author?

JJ: The best thing about being an author is inventing new

worlds and interesting people to populate them. It's also lovely to receive letters from people who have enjoyed the books.

Q: If you inherited a castle, like Katie does in Cloudberry Castle, what would you turn it into?

JJ: I think I would turn my castle into a Writers' Retreat, where authors can finish their books in peace and quiet without the phone ringing.